"Melissa Sinclair called while you were out."

She paused. "She told me that—that your wife is contesting the custody ruling on your daughter. Is that why you married me?"

"I'll do anything to keep my daughter." It was the answer Marie-Claire had dreaded.

"I wish to God I'd married Chris—anybody but you!" She knew a moment of triumph as his face hardened.

"It's too late for regrets," he said bitterly, and strode from the room.

Had it been only hours ago that they had made love so hungrily, with such passion, such need?

Lee had used her as Chris had used her. Even when she'd confronted him with what Melissa had so eagerly revealed, he'd shown no remorse. He had married her because he *needed* a wife... he hadn't even tried to pretend that he loved her.

Books by Patricia Lake

HARLEQUIN PRESENTS

These books may be available at your local bookseller.

For a list of all titles currently available,
send your name and address to:

Harlequin Reader Service
P.O. Box 52040, Phoenix, AZ 85072-2040
Canadian address: P.O. Box 2800, Postal Station A,
5170 Yonge St., Willowdale, Ont. M2N 5T5

PATRICIA LAKE

fidelity

Harlequin Books

TORONTO • NEW YORK • LONDON
AMSTERDAM • PARIS • SYDNEY • HAMBURG
STOCKHOLM • ATHENS • TOKYO • MILAN

Harlequin Presents first edition October 1984
ISBN 0-373-10730-7

Original hardcover edition published in 1984
by Mills & Boon Limited

CHAPTER ONE

UNFORTUNATELY, the long drive from Geneva airport to the station at Täsch gave Marie-Claire plenty of time to think.

The hired car was fast and comfortable and the roads were wide and fairly empty. Even the breathtaking scenery—the snow-clad mountains towering so carelessly around Lake Geneva, the empty though brightly-lit afternoon streets of the towns she sped through—Vevey, Montreux, and on towards Brig—could not take her mind off Chris. Her brain was still exploding with his betrayal, and the expensive, artificially-heated confines of the car seemed to isolate her from the rest of the world, leaving her alone with all those thoughts, making it all too easy to brood. She was trying to escape, but the images filled her mind, refusing to be banished. Her hands clenched on the steering wheel, her eyes blank as she purposefully concentrated on navigating a steep bend ahead. How could he? she thought bitterly. How *could* he?

They had only been engaged for six months, planning to marry the following June. She had trusted him, trusted him completely. There had been no reason for her to do anything else.

She remembered every moment of their time together—once, it had been with happiness and hope, now it was only with bitterness and disgust, his rueful, coaxing smile dissolving her momentary irritation.

He had insisted on paying for the dry cleaning of her skirt, introducing himself as he dabbed ineffectually at the stain with a handkerchief. His blue eyes met hers, filled with apology and laughter, and she had liked him right from that moment.

He was handsome, friendly and open, and she had agreed to have dinner with him the following evening. From then on they had been inseparable. She had been bowled over by his charming, easy-going attitude to life—life that she took rather seriously. Whenever they were together—and as far as Marie-Claire was concerned, they weren't together enough—Chris's job as a journalist could take him out of the country at any time, and frequently did—their time was spent recklessly, excitingly, the hours full of laughter.

'You shouldn't take things so seriously,' he had told her with a half-exasperated smile. 'Grab everything you can—life's far too short to spend time worrying!'

She had laughed, wondering if she could ever do that, hoping she could, promising to try. She had wanted to be like him, had tried to be what he wanted her to be. How naïve, how stupid she had been! Despite her inexperience, how could she have not seen through that easy-going charm to the selfish, shallow man beneath?

When he had very casually suggested that perhaps they should get married, she had been ecstatically happy, sure that he really loved her, agreeing immediately.

He had been amused by her eagerness, almost as though he had never meant to be taken seriously, but too lazy, too uncaring to correct any misapprehensions she might be holding.

And as the months passed, and Marie-Claire gently pressed him into making plans, she had, blinded by the stars in her eyes, deliberately ignored his slight withdrawal, the impatient tightening of his mouth when she shyly demanded decisions.

She had been *so* sure of him. He had asked her to marry him, after all. He loved her, wanted her, respected her enough not to press her into becoming his lover before they were married. She had wanted to wait and he had readily agreed. Whatever she wanted—that had been his favourite phrase. Foolishly she had imagined that it meant he desired only her happiness; now she knew very differently.

That last night she had driven over to his Kensington flat on impulse. She wanted to see him, perhaps they could have dinner together—she had bought some food from the delicatessen. She enjoyed cooking for him.

A hard self-despising smile touched her mouth as she manoeuvred the car through St Niklaus, the last town before Täsch. The road was twisted now, the flat dark countryside far behind. All around she saw tall snow-covered peaks reaching high against the dark yellow evening sky. It was bleaker here, no clusters of wooden chalets in the foothills, no sign of life at all.

Her mind would not stop wandering. She knew now that no man could be trusted, and she hated herself for the easy trusting way she had let herself be taken in by Chris.

Even now her heart still clenched with pain when she remembered arriving at his flat, letting herself in with the key he had given her, singing under her breath.

The lights had been on, the rooms deserted. Perhaps he was taking a shower, she had thought, wandering into his bedroom through the half-open door. She had stopped dead in her tracks. On the rumpled bed, Chris lay making love to another woman.

Both turned as they heard Marie-Claire's stifled cry of amazement, and Chris had smiled ruefully.

'I wasn't expecting you,' he had said, not looking in the least guilty or worried.

'So I can see,' Marie-Claire had replied painfully.

Chris and the woman—Marie-Claire barely looked at her—both laughed, which had seemed the final straw. They made *her* feel the intruder, the awkward fool. Without another word she had run from the flat, numb and desperately miserable, hoping that the whole thing was some terrible nightmare from which she would wake at any minute.

Chris had called to see her the following day. Marie-Claire arrived home from the office where she was temporarily working, after a particularly trying day and a practically sleepless night, to find him sitting waiting for her on the garden wall. He stood up as she approached.

'Hi, what happened to you last night?' She evaded his kiss.

'I came home,' she said shortly, angrily, hurt welling up inside her as the picture of him with that other woman rose before her eyes.

'You're not angry, surely?' He sounded genuinely perplexed, amused.

'Very perceptive!' she snapped, opening the front door.

He followed her inside and she let him, hoping perhaps that he was about to come up with some miraculous reasonable explanation for what she had stumbled upon the night before.

In the lounge he stood watching her, that strange amusement still on his face. Then he said, 'How about dinner tonight?'

Marie-Claire looked into his coaxing handsome face and pain touched her heart.

'No,' she replied, looking away again.

'Oh, come on, darling!' He was moving, trying to

take her into his arms, his voice betraying his surprise. 'Don't sulk, for God's sake, don't sulk!'

'*Sulk?*'

Marie-Claire tore herself away from him, choking with anger and outrage. Incredibly, he didn't care at all, and that hurt more than anything else. As far as he was concerned he needed no excuses for what had happened.

'Sulk? Last night, you . . . you slept with someone else. . . .'

'Sure I did, but there's no need to make such a big deal of it.' He was becoming impatient with her, the amusement fading from his blue eyes.

'I believe in fidelity,' she told him fiercely.

Chris shook his head. 'I've warned you about taking things too seriously.' That laughter was in his voice again, as though she had said something foolishly amusing.

Marie-Claire's eyes mirrored her pain. 'Chris, don't . . . I thought. . . .'

'I never promised you fidelity,' he reminded her coolly. 'And I certainly don't expect you to fly into a jealous wife routine every time I sleep with somebody else.'

Marie-Claire stared at him in speechless, shocked amazement, disillusionment and betrayal crowding in on her, changing everything. That girl last night hadn't been the first, she realised, despising her own naïvety. Fidelity meant nothing to Chris, it was a word that didn't even figure in his vocabulary. And there was no way she could marry a man who wasn't prepared to be faithful to her.

Still angry, she retorted, 'Perhaps we ought to think again about getting married.'

It was a plea for reassurance. Chris had pulled the rug from under her feet and a terrible insecurity was gnawing away at her. Perhaps she had created her own illusion of a Chris who did not exist. Perhaps she had never known the real man.

Sensitive and romantic by nature, she had been filled with dreams of the man she wanted, the man she had thought was Chris.

His words shattered all her final frail hopes as he said casually, 'As you wish. After all, it was you who wanted marriage in the first place, not me.'

Her shock and her insecurity had frozen into fury as he spoke, and she had torn into him then, saying things she deeply regretted later.

Chris had retaliated cruelly and cynically, unable to take her personal criticisms of him. The whole scene had been terrifyingly ugly and had ended with her flinging back his ring. He stooped to pick it up from where it lay, glittering reproachfully on the carpet, and left the house, slamming the door violently behind him.

As soon as he had gone, the pride that had kept Marie-Claire pale, rigid and dry-eyed had evaporated into thin air. Her legs had given way beneath her and she had almost fallen into a chair, suddenly and violently bursting into tears.

It had been the end of all her dreams, her hopes for the future. She was empty and alone and she hated herself. She had been living a self-created lie all the months she had known Chris. She had been deceiving only herself, and the things he had said, though she knew they had been spoken in the heat of anger, hurt her anew as she remembered them.

She had not seen him again after that evening. She had waited and waited hoping he would get in touch, but there had been no word. For herself she did not have the courage to contact him—she was far too afraid of rebuff.

Then, two weeks later, dragged to the theatre by a worried Becky, she had spotted Chris in the foyer. He was with another woman—not even the girl she had caught him in bed with, but a slim ravishing blonde.

His arm was around her shoulders, intimacy cloaked them. As Marie-Claire stared, his eyes suddenly met hers, and the malice she saw in them shocked her. Knowing that she was watching, he bent his head and lingeringly kissed his companion.

Marie-Claire walked away immediately, out into the cold drizzle of the night, blindly looking out for an empty taxi.

She couldn't understand his deliberate cruelty. He hated her, he actually *hated* her!

Becky had followed, concern etched on her face. 'I thought you knew,' she said quietly, touching Marie-Claire's shoulder.

'About Chris's women?' Marie-Claire laughed, high jarring laughter, and Becky looked embarrassed. 'I couldn't say anything,' she began uncomfortably. 'I thought——'

Marie-Claire didn't let her finish. It was more than she could bear this evening. 'Yes, I understand.'

All she wanted was to go home and hide herself away. Her humiliation was unbearable. Everyone had known except her. One day she would show him what he had so carelessly thrown away, although she doubted that he would ever be sorry. . . .

After that disastrous evening it had seemed impossible to stay in London. Her temporary job was coming to an end at Christmas and she had no plans for the holiday.

And then a telephone call from Ran answered her desperate prayers. They were cousins, and he managed a hotel in Zermatt, Switzerland.

They had been close since childhood, Marie-

Claire's parents having been killed in a car crash when she was five. Ran was an only child, and his parents had taken her in, bringing her up as their own daughter.

On the telephone, she half-jokingly asked him if there was any chance of a job in the hotel, over Christmas.

Ran couldn't tell her about the job, but hearing the desperate sadness in her voice, he had insisted she came over to Switzerland immediately.

So here she was, on the day before Christmas Eve, having taken an early afternoon flight from Gatwick, and despite the hollow bitterness around her heart and the fact that for the first time in her life she wasn't looking forward to Christmas, she was longing to see Ran again.

She had not seen him since his father's funeral two years before. Soon after that he had left for Switzerland. He had always been an enthusiastic skier, and had jumped at the job offer.

A year later, Marie-Claire's aunt had remarried and moved to California. Marie-Claire hardly ever heard from her now, which somehow left Ran as her only close family.

Ran had not been at the wedding. His excuse had been pressure of work, but Marie-Claire had known better.

Ran had always been closer to his father, and he found the idea of his mother remarrying very difficult to take. They had all drifted apart since the death of Marie-Claire's uncle. He had been the pin that had held the family together for so many years, and they had never known.

Oh, but she was dying to see Ran, to talk to him, just to be close to him. Her own loneliness was threatening to engulf her.

It was seven o'clock when she reached Täsch, and parking the car in the enormous open car park, she shivered as she stepped out into the bitterly cold wind. It was dark now, and she huddled into the thick fur of her coat, as she pulled her suitcase out of the car boot and made her way towards the brightly-lit ticket office.

Luckily the electric train was due in within a few minutes of her arrival, and she waited in the warmth of the ticket office until she heard the train's metallic roar.

Once on the train she thankfully lit a cigarette, and glanced at her fellow passengers.

Despite the late hour, the train was packed—skiers in bright ski-suits, their tall skis stacked by the tram's automatic doors, a package holiday group with a sporty-looking courier—French, English, German, the languages mingling.

The train from Täsch was the only way into the car-free sports resort, hence its busyness. It was only a three-mile journey, yet it took fifteen minutes,. the train creeping upwards, slowly, carefully, and Marie-Claire had to control her own impatience. She seemed to have been travelling all day.

The freezing cold wind hit her again as she stepped off the train at Zermatt. The station was bright and busy, the air filled with chatter and laughter and the tinkling of bells on the horse-drawn taxis. Christmas trees lined the station roof, twinkling in the darkness, and hotel porters, the names of their hotels on their peaked caps, stood around, waiting for their guests.

Not seeing a porter from the hotel Ran worked at, Marie -Claire enquired from one of the station officials, and found that it was only five minutes' walk from the station.

She had been cramped up in the car and on the plane all day, so she decided to walk.

The hotel was on Bahnhofstrasse, the main street, and she found it easily, its portals bright with enormous Christmas trees.

As she pushed open the doors with her elbow, probably because she was suddenly feeling rather tired, she collided clumsily with a man on his way out. As they cannoned into one another, she caught the impression of immense strength in the hands that grasped her shoulders, steadying her.

Her case fell silently to the thickly-carpeted floor—perhaps it hadn't been such a good idea to walk from the station after all—it had been getting heavier by the second.

She looked up into the man's face, murmuring an apology, her dark eyes freezing in response to the cynical twist of his mouth as he stared down at her.

He was very tall and very dark, the foyer lights gleaming in the blackness of his hair, on the smooth black leather of the coat that emphasised the powerful width of his shoulders.

And in the seconds before she dropped her cold glance, she had the impression of cool grey eyes, of a strong tanned face that seemed all hard planes and angles. A shiver of inexplicable apprehension touched her skin as she reached for her dropped suitcase, but the man was too quick for her.

'Allow me.' His voice was low and attractive, English, or maybe American.

'There's no need——' Marie-Claire began stiffly, but he was already striding away towards the reception desk, and for a few seconds she was riveted by his dark, panther-like grace, before she realised what she was doing, what he was doing. Pursing her lips, anger bright in her eyes, she followed him. Who did he think he was, anyway?

He deposited her suitcase at the desk, and as their

eyes met briefly, he inclined his black head in a mocking silent salute. Then he turned on his heel, leaving the hotel and leaving her reluctantly stammered thanks falling on thin air.

She stared after him for some minutes. He reminded her of somebody . . . there was something about him. It was buried deep in her memory and she couldn't pull it forward. Had they met before? He wasn't the sort of man any woman was likely to forget.

She shook her head. Perhaps he was famous—she could have seen him on the television or at the cinema.

She didn't want to think about him, she didn't want to think about any man. But as she turned away, the strong impression that they *had* met before, and the memory of his cool grey eyes, would not be erased from her mind.

She asked the pretty pale-haired receptionist for Ran. He was in the hotel bar, she was informed, so leaving her suitcase at the desk, she made her way into the bar.

Ran was sitting chatting to the barman. Incredibly he hadn't changed in two years. Or perhaps it wasn't so incredible. Perhaps it was only because her own life was in turmoil that she expected everyone else to have changed with her.

She moved up silently behind him, smiling with affection for him, and placed her small cold hands over his eyes.

'Guess who?' she demanded laughingly.

'Marie-Claire!' He turned to her immediately, taking both her hands in his, kissing her face. 'I didn't expect you today—you should have phoned, I would have met you.'

She returned his kiss, her happiness genuine for the first time in weeks. It was *so* good to see him again. She stared at him, so tall and dark like herself, his face thin, attractive, his clever blue eyes alight with pleasure. He looked younger, even though he was twenty-seven, seven years older than her, fitter and happy.

'I've missed you,' she admitted wryly, unable to stop smiling at him.

'I'm glad you've come,' said Ran, and meant it.

The last time they had talked they had argued. It had been on the telephone, Marie-Claire trying unsuccessfully to persuade him to come to his mother's wedding. Ran was immovable. When he'd taken a decision, he could never be persuaded to change his mind.

They were both remembering that argument now.

'I'm sorry.' She had wanted to say it for a long time.

Ran shrugged, knowing exactly what she was talking about. 'I regret it, you know. I wrote to her and tried to explain——' He looked into Marie-Claire's cold face and said, 'You need a brandy, and after that I'll show you to your room.'

'I——' She hated brandy.

'Don't argue, it's nine degrees below freezing out there tonight. You need brandy.'

She was introduced to Claudio the barman, who had watched their meeting with kind, interested eyes. He was Italian, slim and dark and his glance was openly appreciative on Marie-Claire's pale beautiful face, as he poured a generous measure of brandy.

'Your first visit to Zermatt?' he asked in faintly-accented English.

She nodded, smiling brightly. 'My very first. I hope the natives are friendly!'

Suddenly she was thinking of the man she had collided with on her arrival. There had been nothing friendly about him. Dangerous was the word that sprang to mind.

She chatted with extra effort to Ran and Claudio while she sipped the brandy, that burned her throat and warmed her chilled body, and forced herself to forget the man in the foyer. She had no intention of letting any man intrude into her thoughts or her life. She was finished with all that—utterly determined never to become involved again.

Half an hour later, Ran showed her to her room. It was part of his suite, merited by his position in the hotel, a large room, decorated in warm apricot shades with a thick pale carpet and an en-suite bathroom. The furniture was all light oak, rough and unvarnished, the bed covered in snowy white.

Marie-Claire impulsively kissed his cheek. 'Thanks—for everything.'

She knew that he had recognised her cry for help on the telephone and had immediately responded to it. She was deeply grateful. It restored a little of her faith in human nature.

Ran smiled. 'How about dinner?'

'Yes, I'd like that. I want to talk—you haven't told me any of your news yet,' she said, realising that she hadn't eaten since breakfast, and that seemed years ago.

Ran consulted his watch. 'I'll meet you in the bar in, let's say—an hour?'

'Fine.' Left alone in the room, she wandered around, touching the fabric-covered walls, stepping fleetingly on to the icy balcony.

The view was of mountains, faintly lighter than the dark sky, of tall pine trees and wooden chalet-type houses and hotels. It was picturesque, almost unreal, which somehow matched her mood. It was incredible to realise that she had travelled so far in such a short time—from the grey dirt of London to the pure snowy mountains of Switzerland.

Stepping back into the warmth, she decided to take a hot shower before changing for dinner.

Lifting her suitcase on to the bed, she hung away her clothes in the enormous wardrobes and wandered into the tiled bathroom, undressing as she turned on the shower. The hot pelting water refreshed her, eased the aching muscles that hours of driving had produced, and she let her mind drift blankly as she shampooed her hair.

She dried herself carelessly and allowing the towel to slip to the floor, examined herself curiously in the long steamy mirror. She was tall and slim, her body pale, curved. Her shiny black hair hung to her jaw, swinging thickly in a style that accentuated the delicate bone structure of her face. She had a small gentle mouth and wide dark eyes, her colouring and her name inherited from her half-French mother.

She had been told that she was beautiful many times, but she didn't believe it for a minute. She certainly hadn't been beautiful enough to hold Chris's attention for any length of time, and the shock of the broken engagement had taken pounds off her, leaving her body thinner though, unknown to her, more graceful.

In the bedroom, she carefully made up her face, anxious to disguise from Ran the ravages of sleepless tearful nights, then dressed in a delicate fashionable black silk suit that brought out the dark beauty of her hair and eyes and gave her pale skin a translucent glow. Gold earrings completed the outfit, and switching out the lights, she grabbed her handbag and made her way downstairs to the bar.

Ran was already there, sitting on one of the vast couches arranged around a modern open log fire.

Marie-Claire ordered a gin and tonic and sat down opposite him. 'So, how have you been?' she asked with a smile.

'Busy. We're well into the skiing season now.' He paused, sipping his Scotch. 'About the job, Marie-Claire——'

'Don't tell me, there isn't one,' she cut in wryly, reading his worried expression.

'I'm sorry. We have all the staff we need—and apart from the fact that you don't have the correct papers to work here, I can't fix you up with anything, because the owner flew in a couple of days ago, so we're all on our best behaviour,' Ran explained, still worried.

It was disappointing, but she hadn't really expected there to be a job waiting for her at such short notice.

'It's all right,' she said quickly. 'I wasn't really serious about a job. I know how it is.' She saw him relax, and added, 'I just wanted to see you. Will I be able to stay for a week or two? I'll pay for my room and meals.'

Ran shook his head, laughing. 'There's no need for that. I've explained the situation to Lee and he agrees that the room is yours for as long as you want it—perks of the job. You are my cousin, after all.'

It was a relief. She needed some peace and quiet for a few days.

Finishing their drinks, they strolled arm in arm into the wood-panelled dining room. It looked festive, decorated with golden garlands and shining Christmas trees.

The food was wonderful, four deliciously cooked courses with a choice of dessert, and Marie-Claire found herself eating heartily, enjoying her food for the first time in weeks. To start, there was a smoked fish cocktail, then soup, then salad, then the main course, pork kebabs with noodles and glacé cucumber.

Over coffee and brandy back in the lounge, she was contentedly replete and found herself telling Ran the full story about Chris, unable to keep the bitterness from her voice.

'So you see,' she finished ruefully, 'I've given up the lease on the house I was renting in London and the job is finished, although I knew it was temporary when I took it, so that leaves me very much at a loose end.'

She was glad that the office job was at an end and she had wanted to give up the house as soon as she could. Those things were all part of a life that had included marriage to Chris. And she had desperately wanted to cut free from all ties with that life. It was past, over, and she wanted something completely new to replace it.

Looking back at her hasty actions, she realised that it probably hadn't been such a good idea to burn all her bridges so completely, but at the time, her humiliated pain and her need to get out of the same social circle as Chris, to get out of London altogether, had overridden all other sensible ideas. Ran seemed to understand. He smiled, touching her hand. 'So to sum it up, you're homeless and out of a job, right?'

Marie-Claire laughed. 'That's about it, I suppose.' She felt much happier now she had confided in him. Shared, her problems didn't seem half as bad. 'Anyway, I expect something will turn up, it always does.'

'You can stay here as long as you like. I know I've said it before, but I do mean it,' Ran repeated, still a little worried about her. Marie-Claire had never craved the strange freedom of insecurity. She needed something solid in her life, a need probably born of the loss of her parents so young.

Ran was ordering more coffee for them both when a tall figure appeared before them. It was the man who had picked up her suitcase in the foyer, Marie-Claire realised, as her head jerked up, and again that strange prickle of fear ran down her spine as she looked up at him.

Gone was the fur-lined leather coat and instead he wore a black dinner jacket that somehow seemed to emphasise the tall power of his body, the width of his shoulders.

Ran was smiling. He obviously knew the man.

'Mind if I join you?' the man said in a low, smiling voice.

Ran stood up. 'Of course not, we'd be delighted. Lee, let me introduce my cousin, Marie-Claire Kingsland, Marie-Claire—Lee Harper, my boss.'

She got to her feet gracefully, somehow not surprised that this tall dark, disturbing stranger was Ran's boss, the owner of the hotel. There was something fateful about it all. For a moment she felt as though she no longer had any power over her own destiny.

She held out her hand, and as Lee Harper's strong tanned fingers closed over hers she almost shivered, his touch reaching something inside her.

'How do you do, Mr Harper.' She was polite, but her dark eyes were very cool as they met the expressionless depths of his.

'Miss Kingsland,' he acknowledged softly, his eyes telling her that he saw right through her.

Disturbed, Marie-Claire withdrew her hand as soon as she could, sinking back down into her chair on legs that were strangely weak. What was the matter with her? Surely she wasn't scared of this man?

She glanced at him secretly as he chatted to Ran about some managerial problem that had cropped up.

He was very attractive, she supposed, her usual bitterness welling up. In his mid-thirties, she guessed, he had a strong hard face that spoke of experience, a firm, beautifully moulded mouth and dark grey eyes beneath heavy black brows, eyes that were cool, charming, cynical and unreadable.

She quickly looked away, fingers fiddling with her brandy glass. She didn't want to be near this man. She would make some excuse and escape to her room.

He was looking at her now, she realised with a sudden pang of panic, but pride came to her rescue, lifting her head, and her cold eyes met his almost steadily.

He smiled slightly, his unreadable glance moving slowly from her shining dark head, down over her face, her body, assessing, observing with frankly masculine appraisal, and despite herself Marie-Claire felt the colour staining her cheeks.

Wanting to hide herself from those clever probing eyes, she glared at him.

His smile widened slowly, openly amused by her bristling anger. 'You're on holiday here, I understand, Miss Kingsland.'

She nodded, and catching Ran's worried glance, added as sweetly as she could, for his sake, 'Yes, just for the Christmas holidays—I wanted to see Ran.'

Lee Harper's dark brows rose slightly, his grey eyes effortlessly holding hers. 'Do you ski?'

She shook her head, suddenly wanting to laugh. This polite conversation was so ridiculous!

'No, I must admit I'm not really interested in skiing.' It was meant to put him in his place, but as she looked defiantly into his eyes she saw the humour there, the laughter. It was all a game. He knew exactly what she was trying to do, he also knew that she wasn't succeeding.

Pursing her lips, she rose to her feet. 'If you'll both excuse me,' she said as lightly as she could. 'I seem to have been travelling all day, I'm very tired——'

Both men rose, and the amusement, the knowledge

she saw in Lee Harper's face had her gritting her teeth together. He knew she was running away.

Casting him a poisonous look, she lightly kissed Ran's cheek and made her way stiffly to the lift.

And by the time she got to her room she was *fuming*! What the hell was the matter with her, letting a man like Lee Harper get under her skin? She knew his type—they treated women like playthings. . . . She halted her thoughts. No, that was unfair. She knew nothing about him.

Sitting down on the bed, she kicked off her high-heeled shoes. She did know that he was dangerously attractive. She had felt the pull of his charm, his personal magnetism—she, who was immune to all men now. She was drawn to Lee Harper against her will. True, she had been fighting and kicking all the way, but there was no denying it, and it frightened her to death.

CHAPTER TWO

THAT first night in Zermatt, Marie-Claire had a dream—a strange disturbing dream, and when she woke very early the next morning, she opened her eyes and suddenly knew why Lee Harper had seemed so familiar to her.

It had happened five years ago. She had been fifteen years old, walking home alone from school, lost in a world of her own.

Stepping from the kerb to cross the road, she had not been looking, and had walked straight into the path of an oncoming car. The car had screeched to a halt, missing her by mere fractions of an inch.

She had stood shocked and dazed, unable to move, her long black hair tumbling over her shoulders. And when she had slowly turned her head, she had seen the car door opening and a tall dark man striding towards her.

She had been able to feel his anger as he gripped her arm. He was swearing violently under his breath. She had listened in silence, her dark eyes filling with tears as she stared into his hard furious face. Then suddenly he had stopped shouting and she had heard him sigh. He had been staring at her, taking in her windblown hair, her delicate tear-washed face and slender graceful body.

'Are you okay?' he had asked her quietly. She had nodded mutely.

'Do you want me to drive you home? You're upset—The car didn't touch you, did it?' His dark brows had been drawn together, his voice had been concerned.

Marie-Claire had shaken her head again. 'No,' she had whispered. 'No, I'm fine.'

Then she had smiled at him, a smile of rare radiant beauty. He had stared, his glance sharpening, as though unable to drag his eyes from her.

And then she had walked away, her brain filled with his powerful image. It had been over in minutes, yet she had dreamt of him for many nights after that. His grey eyes had haunted her. He had been a hero, the centre of her fantasies during the following months.

She lay back against the pillows and smiled. Lee Harper, the object of a schoolgirl's dreams. He wouldn't remember, but he'd had a big effect on her.

She laughed out loud. She had been so romantic then, she had actually believed that there was one man in the world for her. Lee Harper had been that man when she was fifteen.

Climbing out of bed, she had the sudden impulse to swim. So, slipping on her bikini under a short towelling robe, she left her room and took the lift down to the basement, where the hotel boasted a heated indoor pool. The place was deserted, the blue water smooth, glinting invitingly against the tiled walls.

Sliding out of her robe, Marie-Claire dived in cleanly, gasping as the cool water touched her skin.

She swam up and down the pool, the exercise toning her muscles, waking her up, until her hunger got the better of her and she climbed out, longing for breakfast. As she reached for her robe, she was aware of someone entering the pool room and, turning, saw with dismay Lee Harper moving towards her, wearing only black swimming trunks and a towel slung carelessly over his shoulders.

Marie-Claire could not drag her eyes away from the

tanned magnificence of his body, so powerfully built, lean and muscular.

She watched him approach, her heart suddenly beating very fast.

'Good morning, Miss Kingsland, you're up and about early,' he said laconically, his grey eyes sliding the length of her curved half-naked body.

'Good morning, Mr Harper,' she replied as blandly as she could manage, struggling into the robe as fast as she could, disturbed by and avoiding his cool gaze.

'You're very beautiful.'

His voice was low, husky, and the hectic colour poured into her cheeks.

'Excuse me——' She turned away in panic, but his hand curled around her wrist, detaining her, not by force but with a warning.

She stared down at his strong tanned fingers, dark against her pale skin, and her heart tripped over itself.

'Let me go . . . .' she whispered, shocked by her own reactions, frightened of them, of him.

'You spend a lot of your time running away, Marie-Claire,' Lee Harper said softly, 'Why, I wonder? I didn't have you marked down as a coward.'

She didn't look at him, she didn't dare. Instead, she fixed her eyes on his shoulders, smooth-skinned, muscular, gleaming. Her mouth was suddenly dry.

'I'm not running away, Mr Harper, I'm merely going to get some breakfast. Swimming always makes me hungry.' Her voice sounded high, breathless, and she cursed herself for what it gave away.

He laughed. 'Look at me,' he commanded quietly.

Stubbornly, Marie-Claire kept her head lowered. She could feel herself trembling and she didn't know why.

'Five years ago, I almost killed you,' Lee Harper drawled quietly, and when her shocked eyes finally met his, he smiled almost cynically. 'You remember?'

She didn't answer, and he continued, 'You took my breath away even then, with your beauty—half child, half woman. You're even more beautiful now.'

'Mr Harper, please . . . I don't know what you're talking about. . . .' she faltered, the lie obvious.

'Liar,' he mocked softly. 'I can see it in your eyes, you remember it as well as I do.'

The fact that she had dreamt about the incident the night before brought a wave of humiliating colour to Marie-Claire's face. She glanced at Lee Harper through her lashes and hated him. She had to get away.

'I suppose you imagine that I have to be polite to you because you're Ran's boss? Is that what you're counting on, Mr Harper?' she demanded icily.

She heard the hiss of his indrawn breath, felt his fingers tightening bruisingly around her wrist. She looked into his face and saw that her remark had hit home, that he was suddenly violently angry.

'I'm counting on nothing, Marie-Claire,' he replied roughly. 'That's a lesson I learned the hard way—a lesson it seems you still have to learn.'

She shivered uncontrollably as he spoke, reading in his cool grey eyes something far deeper than anger, something that trapped the breath in her throat even though she did not recognise it.

'Lee—don't.' She used his name for the first time. They both noticed it as it fell between them.

She flushed, embarrassed, and his eyes darkened, his other hand moving to touch her wet hair. His fingers moved through it, down to the delicate line of her jaw, gently touching her skin, tracing the fragile line of bone.

His dark eyes moved to the swell of her breasts, their rapid rise and fall beneath the wet towelling drawing his gaze.

'Oh, Marie-Claire,' he said deeply, no anger in his voice now, only a strange, smoky roughness, 'there's no way you can fight it, there's no way I'm going to let you fight it.'

She knew what he was talking about. Her whole body was achingly aware of the scorching touch of his fingers, but she pulled away, very frightened, though more of her own reactions than of him.

'No——' she said steadily, her wide dark eyes meeting his, as she drew on every reserve of courage she had. 'No!'

Incredibly, he let her go, and without looking back, Marie-Claire walked towards the lift on legs that felt like jelly.

Safely in her room, she sank on to the bed, her hand over her mouth.

Something had happened down there by the pool. She had looked into Lee Harper's grey eyes and everything had seemed inevitable. Her heart was still pounding. She didn't even know what he wanted from her. She didn't think she wanted to know.

The thought of breakfast made her feel sick, but she found fresh coffee in Ran's sitting room, although no sign of him, so she drank two cups, strong and black. It was amazing that her appetite had disappeared so completely.

What would she do today? she wondered rather miserably. Perhaps it had been a mistake to come to Switzerland. No doubt Ran would be very busy over Christmas—she would probably be on her own for a lot of the time. Wasn't that what she had wanted, though? Some time to sort out the mess she had made of her life. If she was honest, she needed some time alone, and having got it, she ought to make the most of it.

She walked out on to the balcony. It was a fine day, the sky azure blue, the white snow dazzling to the eye.

She gulped in the sharp fresh air and decided to explore the town. At least that would take her away from Lee Harper. She turned back into the warmth. She didn't even want to think about him.

She dressed in jeans, and a thick, brightly-patterned woollen jumper after a quick shower, then pulled on her boots, grabbed her coat and bag and left her room in search of Ran. She found him working on the reception desk in the foyer. He came towards her, his face wry with apology.

'Sorry, love, I'm up to my eyes in it this morning.'

'I can see that,' Marie-Claire smiled affectionately. 'Don't worry, I'm off to explore the town.'

'Have you had breakfast?' Ran was fussing.

'I'm not hungry,' she told him firmly. 'Honestly! Don't worry.'

'Have lunch with me?' he asked, reaching for a ringing telephone.

'Yes,' she agreed immediately.

'Half one, here?'

'Okay.' She pulled on her coat and left him to it. They were obviously madly busy, and yet he didn't seem the least bit flustered. Ran had always been so calm, a pillar of strength during her childhood years. She had always gone to him with her problems, rather than to her uncle. Ran had always helped. Perhaps that was why she had come to him now.

It's about time you stood on your own two feet, she told herself sternly, stepping out into the brilliant morning sunshine. She couldn't expect Ran to come running to the rescue for ever. Her life was in a mess, and it was her own fault.

The view outside soon took her mind off her problems—it was stunning—the ground thick with hard shiny snow, the view of the Matterhorn, high above the town, taking her breath away.

She wandered along the Bahnhofstrasse looking in the shop windows, all far too expensive, she decided, but enjoying it thoroughly. The tiny main street seemed packed with people, some tripping along awkwardly in ski-boots, skis balanced on their shoulders as they made their way to the trains that would take them up to the slopes, and sophisticated women in expensive furs, walking dogs—inhabitants, Marie-Claire decided, as she bought some postcards to send to friends in England.

Mid-morning, she found a tea-room over a pâtisserie, crammed with mouthwatering pastries and chocolate, Swiss specialities.

She pushed her sunglasses on to her head as she climbed the wooden stairs, and taking a table near the window where she could watch the world go by outside, she ordered coffee and began to look through the guide book Ran had given her. She read about the famous mountain guides, the first historic climbing of the Matterhorn by Edward Whymper and his party in 1865. It was fascinating history, and she did not notice the young woman with a small child approaching the table until the woman enquired whether the seats opposite Marie-Claire were taken.

The tea-room had become very busy, Marie-Claire realised, shaking her head and offering the free seats with a smile, before returning her attention to the guide book.

Her reading was cut short, however, as the child, a pretty little boy, suddenly reached across the table, his hand knocking Marie-Claire's half empty coffee cup flying.

'Ricky!' The young woman's face registered dismay, her voice sharp. The child's face immediately crumpled, his blue eyes filling with tears.

'I'm so sorry,' the woman apologised with an embarrassed smile.

'It doesn't matter,' Marie-Claire said reassuringly as she mopped up the staining coffee with paper serviettes. 'It was an accident, he didn't mean to do it.'

The little boy was howling now, his angelic face wet and red and very sweet.

The waitress appeared like magic, efficiently cleaning up the mess in a second, and Marie-Claire ordered another coffee.

'You must let me pay for it,' the young woman cut in quickly.

'No, really——'

'You must.' She was insistent, and Marie-Claire had to give in.

'Thank you.'

'I'm Rima Clarkson, by the way, and the little horror is my son Ricky.' She was beautiful, pale blonde hair curling around her tanned face, her colouring enhanced by the fashionable rainbow-coloured ski-suit she wore.

'I'm Marie-Claire Kingsland.' They smiled at each other. As it turned out, the Clarksons were staying at the same hotel.

'You must have dinner with us one night,' Rima suggested enthusiastically, adding carefully, 'Are you here alone?'

Marie-Claire explained about Ran and Rima revealed that her husband James had gone up to Sunnega with friends, skiing.

'Don't you ski?' Marie-Claire asked curiously.

Rima grimaced. 'Yes, usually, but I wrenched my ankle yesterday, so I'm taking it easy for a few days— hence I'm stuck with Ricky!'

They both laughed, and glanced at the child, who was now stuffing chocolate ice cream into his tiny mouth, tears forgotten.

'He's lovely,' Marie-Claire said wistfully, her

thoughts suddenly filled with Chris and the plans they had had.

She had wanted children—had assumed that Chris would too. Time would probably have proved that assumption as false and as misguided as all her others, she thought acidly.

Looking back, she remembered that Chris had always ignored other people's children. He probably hated them, probably considered them a boring unnecessary restriction of freedom. She closed her eyes, suddenly wincing with pain, and tried to force all thoughts of Chris to the back of her mind.

Promising to meet Rima at the skating rink after lunch—the other girl had the afternoon free as well—Marie-Claire left the tea-room just after twelve and walked back to the hotel, unable to resist looking in the shop windows she passed. They were crammed with the exquisitely carved wooden souvenirs that the region was famous for.

The hotel foyer was warm and quiet, almost deserted, and the dark-haired girl on the reception desk smiled at her as she passed on her way to the lift. When the lift doors opened, she found herself facing Lee Harper.

Flustered, she hesitated, not wanting to get in with him.

'Going up?' His voice was edged with lazy mockery.

Flushing, hating his perception, Marie-Claire strode into the lift, eyes lowered.

He was wearing jeans, tight faded denim that clung to his muscular legs and lean hips, and a soft blue shirt. As the lift silently transported them upwards, she felt Lee's probing grey eyes on her flushed face and didn't dare to look at him.

The lift was taking an interminably long time to reach the ninth floor, where Ran's suite was situated, and she felt trapped, claustrophobic, her heart beating wildly. In the close expensive confines she could smell the clean, male, erotic scent of Lee Harper's body, could see the steady rise and fall of his chest as he breathed.

His hands hung loosely at his sides, and she stared blindly at those long lean fingers, at their tanned strength. For a mindless second she could almost imagine them against her bare skin, the powerful expertise of his touch, the delicate sensual abrasion of hard skin brushing soft skin, and her reaction to those forbidden thoughts was so violent that she shuddered alarmingly.

'Cold?' Lee's voice was unreadable, but she knew without looking that he was still staring at her.

'No, I . . . No. . . .' She didn't know what to say.

'Did you have an enjoyable morning?' he persisted, his voice urbane, smooth.

She looked at him then, wondering why he was bothering with this politeness.

'Very enjoyable, thank you,' she replied stiffly.

He smiled as though she had said something amusing, and she bit her lip, hurt by his laughter, immediately lowering her eyes again.

Lee frowned and reached out, catching her pointed chin in his fingers and forcing her to meet the cool intensity of his eyes again.

She tried to blank out all expression, but it was as though he could read her mind. She knew that he could see the sudden vulnerability she had been trying to hide. And she knew he was about to speak when, miraculously, the lift slowed and the doors slid open.

'My . . . my floor,' she whispered breathlessly, and jerking away from him, rushed from the lift, uncaring what interpretation he might place on her awkward obvious actions.

She was still trembling as she stood in her room, struggling out of her heavy coat.

Lee Harper was a womaniser, his grey eyes spoke of his worldly experience. Why couldn't she act normally with him? Why did she always act like a stupid, terrified teenager? She had met men like him before, she had frozen them off without a thought. She combed her hair with angry hands. She hated him, and in future it must be her top priority to keep out of his way.

Ran was talking to one of the guests when she returned downstairs.

'Wait for me in the bar,' he said, excusing himself from the woman for a moment. 'This shouldn't take long.'

Nodding, Marie-Claire agreed.

Claudio hurried over to her as she sat down on one of the bar stools.

'What can I get you?' His openly appreciative eyes rested on her delicate face.

'Lemonade, please.' She felt like something long and cool.

'You enjoy your stay?' he asked, placing a long frosted glass in front of her.

Marie-Claire smiled. 'Yes, it's lovely here—but expensive, I think.' She was half-teasing.

Claudio raised his hands fatalistically. 'Rich people come here—French, German, American. It is a rich man's town.'

She laughed, sipping the cool lemonade. Claudio served another customer and came back to her.

'You don't ski today?'

Marie-Claire shook her head. 'I can't ski, and learning sounds pretty dangerous—I can't afford any broken bones.'

Claudio shook his head regretfully.

'We have the best skiing in the Alps here. The people who come are serious skiers.'

'Do you ski?' she asked, deciding that she liked him. His eyes caressed her in that age-old Italian way, but she knew she was safe. She was Ran's cousin and Claudio valued his job.

'When I'm not at work, I ski all the time,' he told her with a wide smile.

'Marie-Claire, I'm sorry.' Ran appeared beside her. 'That's the only trouble with this job, whenever I'm in the hotel, I'm assumed to be on duty.'

He ordered a beer, and as soon as Claudio had served it he discreetly disappeared, leaving Ran and Marie-Claire alone.

'Tiring morning?' she asked sympathetically.

'Not really, how about you?'

She told him about meeting Rima Clarkson, but she didn't mention her encounter with Lee Harper in the lift. She didn't know why.

In the restaurant, they ate *viande sêchee,* the wafer-thin strips of air-dried meat that were the speciality of the Valais region, with salad and pickles.

Marie-Claire found herself unable to drag her eyes away from a young couple seated near them, obviously deeply in love with each other.

Ran touched her hand when she didn't respond to a question he had asked. 'Don't,' he said quietly.

'They look so happy,' she said, looking away.

'It'll happen to you one day,' he promised, smiling.

'It already has, and it was a disaster.' She tried to hide her bitterness.

'I know this is the standard line, but honestly, you will get over it, meet someone else, someone who's right for you.'

She tried to smile back at him. He was so kind. 'Will I? I can't believe it.'

'You'll see.' He sounded very sure.

'What about you?' she asked curiously. 'Is there anyone for you, Ran?'

His eyes dropped from hers and she wondered if she shouldn't have asked. Before he had moved out here, Ran had had many girl-friends, none of them particularly serious.

'There was someone,' he admitted, a faint flush along his high cheekbones as he sipped his wine. 'A guest.'

'Didn't it work out?' she probed gently, surprised because he had never mentioned it in letters or phone calls.

Ran shook his head. 'I never really had a chance. It was last year, she stayed all summer, but—well, she was married. I couldn't help myself—I think I fell in love with her the moment I saw her.'

Marie-Claire's heart went out to him. Ran had always hidden his deepest feelings, it was part of his character.

'Is there no chance?' she asked sadly.

'She's gone back to the States, I don't suppose I'll ever see her again,' he replied with a shrug of his shoulders.

'Oh, Ran, I'm so sorry!' They understood each other so perfectly and she knew how he must be feeling.

'I'm getting over it, so don't worry.' He smiled, but Marie-Claire knew it was an effort.

'It's so unfair!' she burst out, unable to bear the injustice of love. Ran deserved to be happy. He was everything any woman could want—kind, considerate, intelligent, attractive.

'Life's unfair,' he reminded her, pulling a face, his voice amused. That made her laugh and eased her sadness a little. She knew the last thing he wanted was her feeling sorry for him.

'You've certainly made an impression on the boss,' Ran remarked casually over coffee, some time later.

Marie-Claire's heart lurched. 'What?' she asked inanely, carefully replacing her cup in its saucer so that he should not see the sudden trembling of her hands. Pull yourself together, she thought sternly.

'Interested?' He was teasing her.

'Ran, what on earth are you talking about?' She tried to sound lightly exasperated, but her eyes were suddenly very large in her small face.

'He was asking a lot of questions about you this morning,' Ran revealed, watching her carefully.

'What sort of questions?'

'Oh, you know, the usual stuff—married? engaged?—a conquest, I think, Marie-Claire my dear.'

'Did . . . did you tell him about Chris?' she asked anxiously.

'Of course not. I just told him that you're single, footloose and fancy free.'

'Surely he can't be——?'

'Interested? Why not? You're very beautiful.' Ran smiled at her. She had always been totally unaware of her own beauty.

'Thank you, but I'm not *that* beautiful,' she replied worriedly.

'You underestimate your appeal,' Ran said wickedly. 'You've certainly got the boss hooked!'

'Well, the feeling is not reciprocated,' she retorted emphatically.

'No?' His teasing scepticism made her flush and he pounced on that eagerly. 'I knew it!'

'All right,' she admitted very grudgingly. 'All right, I am curious about him, I suppose, but only because——'

She searched her mind for a good reason and couldn't come up with one. Why should she care whether or not he was interested in her? She certainly had no designs on him. She didn't want involvement with anybody after Chris. But she did want to know about Lee Harper, perhaps because he produced such a violent reaction in her. That was another mystery.

'Because?' Ran prompted, his mouth curving at her genuinely puzzled expression.

Marie-Claire shrugged. 'All right, I don't know. But tell me anyway.'

'What do you want to know?'

She had the feeling Ran was trying to play Cupid. Well, it wouldn't work with Lee Harper. If there was one thing Marie-Claire knew without being told, it was that Lee Harper would not be pushed into anything by anybody.

'Ran——' she began warningly.

His face was innocent. 'You asked,' he protested, his eyes bright with laughter.

'So, tell me all the gossip and then we'll leave it at that, right?'

'Right.'

She could see that she was getting nowhere, but couldn't help smiling.

'He owns this hotel, yes?' she began tentatively, and was shocked to realise that she was in fact *very* curious about Lee Harper, very curious indeed.

'Not only this one,' Ran corrected. 'He owns two other hotels in Zermatt and I believe he's got hundreds of them worldwide.'

'*Hundreds?*' She was surprised.

'You'd better believe it—he's a very wealthy, very powerful man. The multi-millionaire hotel owners hold a lot of power in Switzerland. Just because he's human, don't let that fool you. Lee Harper can pull any strings he wants to.'

The fact that Lee Harper was incredibly rich and

incredibly powerful frightened her a little, but somehow did not satisfy her curiosity. She was more interested in the man himself. She had been able to guess, just by looking at him, that he had money and power.

'Okay, I get the message. What else?' she asked with interest.

'Nobody knows all that much about him,' Ran informed her, racking his brains. 'He's a very private man. Oh, yes, he's got a beautiful daughter—she's about six now, I think.'

Marie-Claire was hardly listening. As soon as Ran had said the word 'daughter' her heart had plunged into her stomach.

'He's married, then?' she said, with as much coolness as she could muster. She should have known men like Lee Harper were never free. And if he was married, what the hell had he been playing at earlier that morning?

'Divorced,' Ran supplied succinctly. 'So you're in with a chance, my child.'

Marie-Claire smiled to herself. It was a relief, she couldn't deny it. Jumping to conclusions again, she thought, mentally ticking herself off.

'Mind you,' Ran continued unabashed, 'you've got a lot of competition—the gossip columns are full of women who would tear each other apart to get to him.'

'Ah, a womaniser,' Marie-Claire said with distaste. 'I might have known!'

'I don't think so. Women do seem to find him irresistible, lucky bastard, but I wouldn't put him down as a womaniser.' Ran's respect for the man was obvious.

'What else?' She was openly avid now.

'As I say, I don't know much about him. I like him—he's got a brilliant mind, he's fair, he pays well—and what more could a good employee want?'

'Well, thanks for the information.'

'Oh, and while we're on the subject,' Ran suddenly cut in, 'be nice to him, will you? Please? For my sake? I got the distinct impression that you were about to ruin my chances of promotion last night, and I really can't afford that.'

'You said he was fair!' she protested laughingly.

'And so he is, but if you're what he wants, you'd better be on my side. Which reminds me, he's given me some time off over Christmas, so we'll be able to spend some time together—I'll show you round.'

'Great! I was beginning to feel a bit lonely,' she admitted ruefully. 'Oh, I know, don't say it—it's all my own fault for foisting myself on you at such a busy time.' She smiled at him. 'I have missed you, Ran.'

He took her hand. 'And I you. I'm glad you've come.'

He was busy that afternoon, so after lunch Marie-Claire strolled round to meet Rima at the skating rink.

The sun was hot, even though the air was so cold, and she couldn't take her eyes off the Matterhorn. It was so big, so majestic, and it seemed so near, she almost felt that if she walked to the outskirts of the town, she would find herself at the foot of the mountain, when in fact it was miles and miles away. It was difficult to get perspective in a place like this.

Down one side of the ice rink was a long wooden chalet, outside it, tables and chairs. It seemed a popular meeting place, for most of the tables were taken.

Marie-Claire weaved her way among the chairs, her boots clattering on the wooden boards. Rima and Ricky had already arrived, and Rima was drinking coffee.

It was pleasant to sit in the sun, sipping hot coffee and watching the skaters, who ranged from clumsy beginners to fantastically accomplished professionals, and Marie-Claire found herself relaxing. Rima was good company, witty and clever and obviously very happy. Some time during the lazy afternoon, Ricky fell asleep and the two girls chatted on, a friendship growing between them almost immediately.

Marie-Claire learned that Rima's husband James was an executive in the oil business and that they had spent their last two Christmases in Zermatt, anxious to get out of London's wet grim greyness during the festive season.

'Christmas means snow for me,' Rima said laughingly. 'So where better than Switzerland?'

And it was while they were talking the hours away that wide powerful shoulders suddenly blocked out the sun.

Marie-Claire heard Rima's exclamation of pleasure as the man bent to kiss her cheek, then sat down next to her. His eyes met Marie-Claire's. It was Lee Harper.

CHAPTER THREE

THE waitress was at his side immediately and Marie-Claire heard him ordering coffee for all of them. She bent her head, allowing the black silk of her hair to fall over her suddenly flushed cheeks.

'I thought you'd be on the slopes,' said Rima, smiling at him broadly.

'Not today.' Lee's voice was low and cool, and Marie-Claire knew he was watching her. 'I had some business to attend to.'

'You know Marie-Claire, of course?' Rima was watching her now, as well. She had to act normally.

'Yes.'

His one-word answer held a wealth of meaning that knotted Marie-Claire's stomach with tension, and gathering every ounce of composure she had, she lifted her head and met his eyes.

'We met yesterday,' she acknowledged evenly, as the waitress set fresh coffee before them.

'How's the ankle today?' Lee asked Rima, and there was a gentle charm in his face, as though they had been friends for years.

'Better, but not better enough,' Rima replied with a grimace. 'James is up at Sunnega, the pig!'

'You won't have to wait long,' Lee told her, his eyes meeting Marie-Claire's, as though the statement was directed at her. She could read a double meaning into everything he said. Overreaction, she told herself, but she watched him covertly as he chatted to Rima, watched the casual lift of his broad shoulders beneath the jacket he wore, watched the muscles contracting in his brown throat as he swallowed back his coffee, and felt the deeply compelling urge to touch him. There was no point in denying that to herself any longer.

And she could affect him just as deeply, she knew that; their awareness of each other was electric, it could cut them off from the rest of the world.

Even now, whenever their eyes met casually, they were alone, Rima, with her bright clever chatter, fading away completely.

That was what frightened Marie-Claire. She had recognised it the moment they collided in the foyer. Five years ago she had wanted him with a terrifying adolescent need. She still wanted him, yet because of Chris's betrayal, she couldn't trust him.

She wanted to be like Chris, she wanted to be like her friends who indulged in casual passionate affairs.

She was drawn to Lee Harper however hard she fought it. Why shouldn't she take from him what she wanted, as he had no doubt taken from countless other women?

She turned away from the thought of him with other women and didn't want to know why.

She looked at him. His eyes were screwed up against the sun, at their corners, a web of tiny lines etched his tanned skin. She wanted him, she couldn't fool herself about that. She was a liberated woman, she thought fiercely. If she didn't take what she wanted, she would spend the rest of her life regretting it, being used by people like Chris. It was a hot, exciting decision, it was what she needed.

So she smiled at Lee Harper, her dark eyes gentle, mysterious. 'Ran tells me you have a daughter, Mr Harper,' she said lightly, sensing the sudden stillness in him at her unexpected smile.

'Lee,' he corrected, an answering smile curving his firm mouth.

'Lee,' she repeated obediently, her voice faintly husky.

'Yes, Laurie is spending Christmas with her mother,' he said expressionlessly.

'It's such a shame she's not with you,' Rima cut in, blindly unaware of the roaring tension between Marie-Claire and Lee. 'She loves it so much here.'

'Naomi wanted her, in fact she insisted,' said Lee, his eyes never leaving Marie-Claire.

Rima followed the direction of his glance and as she looked from one to the other, the penny dropped.

'Time I fed the little horror,' she announced, getting to her feet. 'Otherwise I won't get a moment's peace!'

Marie-Claire made a move too, but Rima waved her hand negatively. 'Stay and finish your coffee,' she insisted. 'I'm sure Lee will escort you back to the hotel—won't you, darling?'

'It would be my pleasure,' Lee said smilingly, adding, 'You'll never make an actress, Rima.'

As she kicked off the brake on the pushchair she shrugged, turning back to them, eyes dancing. 'Who wants to? I'm a happily married woman!'

Laughing, they watched her go. 'She's so nice,' Marie-Claire said softly.

'Yes, she is,' Lee agreed, watching her intently. 'But you're beautiful, Marie-Claire—dammit, I can't take my eyes off you!'

Marie-Claire flushed, her heart beating irregularly. 'Lee, don't. . . .' she whispered, almost in panic. She was overwhelmed by him, afraid of what she had unleashed between them. When she met his darkening eyes she was lost, shattered by what she read there, unable to fully comprehend what had happened, how it had happened in such a short time.

She pretended to watch the skaters. The rink was

emptier now as the sun faded, and the mountains became hazy, shrouded in late afternoon mist.

'Why did you change your mind?' Lee asked quietly.

She bit her lip nervously, the panic beating through her body again. 'I . . . well, I. . . .'

'Don't be afraid,' he said, a soft roughness in his voice as he stared at her vulnerable profile.

'I can't help it,' she whispered honestly.

'Have dinner with me tonight,' he said quietly, and when her head spun round, he added with wry gentleness, 'It's okay, Rima and James will be there, Ran, and a couple of other people.'

'In that case, yes,' her voice was quick and nervous and light, 'I'd love to.'

'Let's walk.' He took her hand, and as they walked past the other tables she was aware of women looking at Lee, assessing him, obviously impressed. She felt the touch of his hard lean fingers around hers like a brand, it left her feeling strangely weak.

They walked towards the church. Lee was silent, his face unreadable as he walked beside her, deliberately slowing his pace to match hers.

As the light faded, the skiers came down from the hills, tiny dark figures shooting across the snow in neat lines of descent.

Watching them, Marie-Claire suddenly lost her footing on the tightly packed ice beneath her. She felt herself falling, and a gasp of shock escaped her. Then she felt Lee's strong arms reaching for her, pulling her against his hard body as he steadied her. She found her face only inches away from his, his hands holding her safe.

'I didn't do that on purpose,' she murmured, hot colour staining her cheeks because she felt so foolish. It was such an age-old, stupid ploy. She would never have dreamed of trying it, yet he couldn't possibly believe that it had been an accident.

'I know,' Lee's slight smile was incredibly gentle, but as she looked into his grey eyes, she saw a rough shadowed darkness belying that smile.

'Really?' It was silly, but she had to be sure.

'I know you don't play games,' he said, his voice faintly harsh. He was still holding her, so closely she could see the muscle jerking spasmodically in his jaw. Her eyes rested on it in fascination.

'Lee——'

She was stopped by his mouth as it touched hers with a hunger that overwhelmed them both. If she had imagined the touch of his lips, it was nothing compared to the reality. She clung to him, lost to everything as his strong hands framed her face, his mouth deeply searching hers.

Then all too soon he released her. She opened dazed eyes to find them staring down at the parted contours of her lips.

'Five years is a hell of a long time,' he muttered softly, his warm breath fanning her cheek.

Marie-Claire laughed, a dizzy excitement coursing through her veins. He wanted her. She could see the tense self-control in the lines of his powerful body and the tautness of his mouth. It was a sweet power to hold, all the sweeter because her need was as great as his, fanned into an aching weakness by the fierce touch of his lips.

'Why do you laugh?' he asked indulgently, stroking back her hair from her face.

'I'm happy,' she admitted, her smile brilliant. And for the first time in weeks, it was true. In Lee's company, she could forget everything sad, everything that hurt her. He acted on her mind and body like some powerful drug, she was aware only of him and the snowy unreal beauty of her surroundings.

'It's good to see you smile.' The deep warmth in his voice shivered along her spine. He took her hand again and they continued walking through the thick snow, across the icy, fast-flowing river on a tiny bridge that overlooked the neat little graveyard. Back on the Bahnhofstrasse, all the shops were brightly lit, the Christmas trees sparkling gold, making the sky darker above the high buildings.

The main street was packed with people, alive with noise and chatter, the smell of roasting chestnuts tantalising Marie-Claire's nostrils.

Lee slid his arm around her shoulder, pulling her closer to his hard body. People stopped to greet him, shouting across the narrow street in French, German or English. Lee spoke fluently in all languages, introducing her to the people they met.

She watched him talk; she couldn't drag her eyes away from the magnetic charm of his smile. He was cool and clever, and she watched people's reactions to him—the men respectful, friendly, the women smiling, their eyes inviting.

'You know everybody,' she said, smiling at him too.

Lee bent his dark head, his mouth brushing her forehead. 'It's a small town,' he said laughingly, but she knew that he was understating his influence here.

Tucked away off the main street was a tiny flower shop with steamy windows, where Lee bought her what seemed like hundreds of red roses. His grey eyes were serious as he gave them to her and she felt her heart lurching violently.

'Thank you,' she whispered, inexplicably close to tears, burying her face in their scented velvet beauty. Christ had never bought her flowers. No man had.

'They were supposed to make you happy,' said Lee with wry gentleness.

'They're beautiful.' Her dark eyes were shy and strangely innocent as they met his. 'I'm just being silly.'

Lee read the sadness in her pale face. Someone had hurt her badly, and his jaw clenched. If he ever got his hands on the bastard—God, was he going crazy?

'Come on.' He slid his arm around her shoulders again and they stepped into the deep pink evening outside.

'It's snowing!' Marie-Claire breathed with delight, watching the powdery flakes drifting slowly to the ground. 'And it's Christmas Eve!' She grabbed his arm, almost unaware of what she was doing. 'Oh, Lee, isn't it beautiful!'

He stared down into her radiant little face, transformed from the sadness of a few moments before. 'Yes,' he said harshly. 'Marie-Claire——' He put his hands on her shoulders, gently turning her to face him.

She smiled up into his serious grey eyes, suddenly fiercely and brilliantly happy. 'What?'

'I want you,' he said huskily. The words shuddered through her, weakening her whole body with an aching heat.

'I want you too,' she whispered honestly, innocently provocative. When she looked into his shadowed eyes she could not deny him the truth. She felt as though she was in a different world here in Switzerland. The sheer beauty of the place gave her a feeling of unreality. This was a different Marie-Claire Kingsland, who told Lee Harper that she desired him.

She was free and happy and honest, and deeply attracted to the tall dark man who stood before her. She had shed her skin like a snake, tired of being hurt, tired of feeling miserable and unhappy. Here, she could be a different person, the real Marie-Claire who lived in her heart, who lived free of society's inhibitions, to her own rules and not other people's. Here she was strong and self-sufficient, not submissive and yielding. Here she could take what she wanted. And she wanted Lee Harper.

She felt Lee's fingers tightening on her shoulders, heard the hiss of his indrawn breath.

'Don't be serious,' she begged. She wanted this heady freedom to last for ever, and if Lee was serious, she might have to face the old harsh reality again. She wasn't ready for that, she had only just found her shaky new happiness.

Lee read her eyes easily, and a slight frown darkened his face. He couldn't push her, yet he couldn't let her walk into this with her eyes closed. It was too important for either of them to have any illusions.

'Don't be serious,' she repeated softly, and he shook his head, half smiling at his own desire to rush things.

He would have to be patient for the first time in his life, he couldn't reach out and take what he wanted. If he did that, he would lose.

Five years was a long time, almost too long to wait for a woman who had had no idea of his existence.

They walked slowly back to the hotel, Lee watching Marie-Claire's entranced face as they moved out of the way of the horse-drawn sleighs with their ringing, jangling bells, and the tiny electric taxis that shot through the snowy streets.

The atmosphere was festive, the shops warm and inviting, decorated richly for Christmas. Marie-Claire felt so happy she was floating, sure that it was only the strength of Lee's arm draped possessively around her shoulders that stopped her drifting skywards.

Ran was on the reception desk as they entered the hotel, his surprised eyes meeting Marie-Claire's as he took in her flushed face, Lee's arm around her, and the enormous bunch of red roses.

They stopped to say hello and Marie-Claire was introduced to Conradin Lüthy, the assistant manager, small and slim with dark eyes and heavily-accented English, of which he was obviously very proud.

He would be taking over while Ran took some time off. Marie-Claire could see Ran burning up with curiosity and she smiled at him, her eyes promising to explain later.

In the lift, Lee silently trapped her against the wall, his arms at either side of her. She looked into his dark, hard-boned face and murmured his name. He slowly bent his head, his glittering gaze fixed on her mouth, and she closed her eyes as his lips brushed the parted softness of hers.

She sighed, that aching need she now recognised as desire, running through her veins, but his kiss was tantalisingly brief, and the lift stopped at her floor all too soon.

In her room, she shrugged out of her coat and kicked off her boots, then carefully put the roses in water. She still felt dazed, all her actions gracefully slow.

She had two hours until dinner, so she picked up the telephone at the side of the bed and ordered some coffee, a smile curving her gentle mouth. Christmas Eve—a day that had started with such little promise, and now seemed unbreakable in its happiness.

She stared at the perfect roses, her thoughts filled with Lee. It was a cliché, but she really had never felt like this before. It was totally beyond her experience.

The light tapping on the door broke into her reverie, and she found Ran outside, holding a tray of coffee.

'First-class service,' she teased laughingly, stepping back to let him in.

'You know why,' said Ran, watching her as he set down the tray on the table.

Marie-Claire curled herself up on the huge leather sofa and shot him an innocent look. 'You nosy thing,' she said, pouring coffee for them both.

He laughed, 'You're not going to tell me, are you?'

She smiled mysteriously. 'Aren't my flowers beautiful?'

Ran didn't answer.

'All right, what do you want to know?' she asked, nibbling at one of the tiny sandwiches he had brought with the coffee.

'Well, as I recall, at lunch,' he looked at his watch, 'only a few hours ago, you weren't all that interested.'

'You told me to be nice to him,' Marie-Claire protested teasingly.

'Oh, I see, you're sacrificing yourself for me,' Ran said laughingly.

'I've changed my mind—I like him, and I've decided that from now on I'm going to follow my own intuition—that can't be wrong, can it?'

Ran smiled. 'No, I guess not. It's good to see you laughing again.'

It meant a lot to her that Ran approved. 'You know we're invited to dinner tonight?'

Ran nodded. 'Seven-thirty, isn't it?'

They finished their coffee, chatting companionably. Even after all this time they had fallen back so easily into their old, close friendship, and that mattered a great deal to Marie-Claire.

She took a long hot bath before getting ready for dinner, letting her mind drift as she lay in the steaming scented water. She already knew what dress she would be wearing—red silk from the 1920s, a simple style with narrow shoulder-straps and a low waistline. It had been left to her by her French grandmother, and it was her favourite dress, the rich colour enhancing her dark beauty.

Stepping from the bath, she dried her hair and brushed it until it shone, then carefully made up her face, paying particular attention to her eyes.

That done, she slipped into the red silk dress and dabbed her pulse spots with a tiny amount of her favourite perfume. She had just decided that jewellery was unnecessary, when Ran knocked on her door.

'Ready? Lee appreciates punctuality——' He stopped, whistling under his breath. 'My God, you look stunning!' he exclaimed, eyeing her from head to toe.

'Thank you,' she smiled, pleased. 'You look pretty dashing yourself.'

And he did, in black evening dress, his shirt immaculately white.

'Shall we go?' He offered her his arm.

'I'm so nervous,' she admitted, as the lift carried them up to Lee's penthouse suite.

'Nobody who looks as lovely as you do should be nervous,' Ran told her gallantly.

Marie-Claire squeezed his arm. 'You're so kind,' she said, her eyes misting stupidly.

And her nerves felt unbearably stretched when the lift doors opened. Lee was waiting for them, his grey eyes devouring Marie-Claire as he shook hands with Ran. They laughed together over something Lee said, then Ran disappeared inside, leaving Marie-Claire, her heart beating like thunder in her ears, facing Lee.

'Marie-Claire——' He murmured her name deep in his throat, moving lithely towards her, tall and powerful in a deep blue velvet dinner jacket and black trousers, his dark hair brushed back, gleaming, thick and vital, his tanned, hard-boned face serious as he took her hand, raising it to press his lips to the small palm.

'You look beautiful,' he murmured against her skin.

She shivered, speechless as she gazed into the smoky grey depths of his eyes.

'Thank you,' she managed, the compliment burning pleasurably in her mind.

Taking her arm, he led her into an enormous lounge that seemed filled with people.

'What will you have to drink?' he asked with a slight smile.

'A gin and tonic, please.' She watched his every movement as he fetched it for her. She stared at his lean brown hand curled around the crystal glass, a terrible need building up in her as the moments passed.

Rima and James Clarkson had already arrived. James was tall and ruggedly attractive, his greying hair distinguished. He was pleasant, charming and Marie-Claire took to him immediately. She also liked James' niece Bettina, who was with them. Bettina was small and blonde and dressed in pale blue taffeta, and her eyes could scarcely be dragged away from Lee. She was attracted to him, Marie-Claire realised, feeling a sharp pang of what could only be called jealousy, as Lee smiled at the blonde girl.

The last two guests arrived as Marie-Claire stood chatting to Ran and Bettina, a couple in their early thirties, Marie-Claire estimated. They were introduced as Tanya and Rafael Canovas.

She was English, breathtakingly beautiful, her dress revealing green crêpe-de-chine, her vivid red hair curling around a sharply feline face. Rafael Canovas was tall and slim and very handsome with dark flashing eyes, and he held Marie-Claire's hand a little too long when they were introduced.

Marie-Claire watched Tanya, her polished nails against the soft velvet of Lee's jacket. She was flirting with him unashamedly. Lee was being polite, charming.

Marie-Claire turned away, asking Rima about Ricky. She did not want to see.

They ate dinner round a huge oval table, shining with silver and crystal. Marie-Claire found herself next to Lee, with James Clarkson at her left.

The food was wonderful. They began with pâté, followed by consommé Royale, then salad with a bitter-sweet dressing and oeuf poché Bénédictine. The main course was veal cooked in thyme with carottes glacés and haricots verts. It was beautifully prepared, served by silent waiters and by the time dessert was set before them—a rich chocolate and banana tart— Marie-Claire was happily replete.

During the meal, Tanya Canovas prettily but relentlessly demanded Lee's attention.

Looking at her, Marie-Claire knew that she could never compare with Tanya's sparkling beauty, her seductive charm. She looked away again, suddenly miserable. Why had she ever thought she had anything to offer a man like Lee?

Masking her insecurity, she chatted to James, noticing that Ran and Bettina were getting on very well together. But she couldn't stop herself listening to Lee's deep voice as he effortlessly charmed his guests.

Back in the lounge, they sat on pale leather sofas and drank coffee and brandy; and Marie-Claire found herself cornered by Rafael Canovas, who stared at her slender body with smouldering soulful eyes.

She fended him off easily, laughing at his barely-veiled suggestive remarks and wondering what sort of a marriage he and his wife had. They had barely spoken two words to each other since their arrival, and Tanya had spent every moment she could wangle with Lee.

Suddenly there was music, and Bettina and Ran were dancing in front of huge panoramic windows.

'I can't believe that you don't belong to someone,' Rafael murmured, leaning towards her with what he imagined was an irresistible smile. 'No husband? No fiancé?'

A shadow of pain flickered in her eyes, although she was aware that he couldn't know.

'I shall only marry for money, Mr Canovas,' she told him with a brilliant smile, and turned her head to find Lee standing just behind her, his face dark, his mouth tight with anger.

'Would you care to dance?' he asked, his eyes holding hers.

Marie-Claire hesitated, her new-found freedom and confidence wavering a little. If she got involved with him, wasn't she asking to be hurt the way Chris had hurt her?

'Marie-Claire?'

She looked up and couldn't resist him. She got to her feet and allowed him to take her hand, aware that Tanya's narrowed green eyes were following them every inch of the way.

She·felt his arms come around her as they began to move to the slow, sensual music. She was trembling with his nearness, her heart pounding. He was staring down at her, but she didn't dare to look at him, and when the hardness of his thigh brushed her, it took all her self-control to stop herself jumping.

'Did you mean what you said about marrying for money?'

She could feel his cool breath against her hair. She looked at him then, her eyes blank. 'Why not? Can you think of a better reason for getting married?'

Lee smiled, his arms tightening around her slender body. 'How about love?' he suggested softly.

'I don't think I believe in love,' she replied, and knew she was lying. She was already more than halfway to being in love with him.

'You're not a cynic, Marie-Claire, I can see those dreams in your eyes, they shine like stars. So I can only assume that it's Rafael's persistent hunting——'

'Or his wife's,' she cut in with a sweet smile.

Lee's dark brows rose and his eyes were lazy with amusement. 'Are you jealous, my love?'

'Are you?' she parried, shivering slightly in his strong arms.

'Oh, yes, I'm jealous,' he admitted, a soft violence threading his voice. 'Dammit, I'm jealous of every man who looks at you!'

The possessive darkness in his eyes made her heart lurch. 'Do you believe in love?' she asked curiously.

Lee's mouth brushed her sensitive earlobe.

'Yes,' he said very softly against her skin.

Shaken, Marie-Claire bent her cheek to his wide shoulder and let her body relax against his, hearing the faint hiss of his indrawn breath as she did so.

In his arms everything was all right again, and as the evening passed, people began drifting away. Rima and James were the first to leave, followed by Tanya and Rafael Canovas, Tanya shooting Marie-Claire a poisonous look as she strode gracefully from the room.

Marie-Claire almost laughed and finished her brandy, smiling at Ran, who she knew had been watching the whole thing.

Her eyes followed Lee. He was the perfect host, charming, witty, charismatic, God, how she wanted him!

And when Bettina and Ran left arm in arm, they were alone, the music louder now because of the silence.

Moving indolently across the room, Lee sat down next to her, loosening his tie. She didn't look at him, her stomach knotted with sudden heat and tension.

'Do you want another drink?' he asked quietly.

'No. No . . . I ought to be going . . . .' she whispered, her mouth dry.

'I'll escort you to your room,' he smiled, getting to his feet in one easy graceful movement. Marie-Claire watched him through half-closed eyes, all at once too tired to move. 'Can I ask you a question?' she said quietly.

Lee stared down at her, his eyes narrowed. 'Sure.'

It was something she had to know, even though she was scared to ask. 'I know . . . I know it's none of my business, but . . . but. . . .' Screwing up all her courage, she finished quickly, 'Are you and Tanya Canovas lovers?'

Lee's dark eyes held hers, the grey depths serious. 'No, and we never have been lovers,' he replied truthfully.

'Have I offended you by asking? I mean, it's not the sort of thing I should have asked, I know. It's very personal . . . but. . . .' She bit her lip, very scared, but desperately relieved.

Lee took her hands and pulled her to her feet, against his body.

'You haven't offended me, Marie-Claire.'

Suddenly their faces were very close as she tried to regain her balance, and acting on an impulse she could not control, she reached up and tentatively traced the hard lines of his face.

She felt the tightening of his jaw under her exploring fingers, the hardness of his cheekbones, and smiled sleepily.

'Lee——' The word was lost as his mouth found hers, parting her lips hungrily, his arms closing tightly around her, crushing her to the hard power of his body. His kiss deepened, drugging her with pleasure, and her hands moved to his wide shoulders, fingers clenching against the tense unyielding muscles beneath the soft velvet of his jacket.

He was so strong, she thought achingly, gasping as his mouth trailed fire to the vulnerable line of her throat, arching back her head to allow him access to her skin. His lips were at her bare shoulders now, pushing aside the straps of her dress, his tongue erotically tracing the fragile line of her collarbone.

Marie-Claire shivered, desire beating hotly in her body, melting achingly in the pit of her stomach, weakening her legs so that she had to lean against him or fall.

When Lee finally raised his head and their eyes met, his glittered with sensual awareness.

Marie-Claire swayed towards him, her own eyes shadowed with the intense emotion she was feeling, and she heard him groan under his breath, his mouth parting hers again, this time with a fierce need that had her yielding completely, matching his passion with an innocent hunger of her own. She was dimly aware of his arms sliding beneath her, lifting her on to the huge soft sofa, and she eagerly arched against him as he moved over her, his deft fingers pushing down the red silk dress to expose the soft thrust of her breasts.

Her own hands were moving too, of their own volition, pushing the soft velvet from his powerful shoulders, fumbling with the buttons of his shirt until his hard brown chest with its matt of fine dark hair, was beneath her trembling fingers.

She moaned as Lee touched her breasts, and a white-hot pleasure shot through her, her nipples hardening, aching beneath his deliberate delicate touch. No man had ever touched her so intimately or with such hungry expertise. No man had ever aroused her to such a feverish pitch.

His dark smouldering gaze blazed across her white skin, he stared down at her swollen breasts, before his mouth touched hers briefly, tormentingly, sliding the length of her throat, across her slim shoulders and down to her bare breasts. She shuddered, hardly able to breathe, her hands flat against his warm hair-roughened chest as he teased her hardened nipples with his tongue, his teeth, his lips.

She heard him huskily murmuring her name, his face buried in the scented hollow between her breasts, then she felt him stiffening his body with immense self-control, and as he moved away, she felt the cool air touching her bare skin.

She opened her eyes to find him fastening his shirt, pushing the silky material back into his trousers with tense quick hands. She frowned, confused. Didn't he want her now? Had she done something wrong?

Hot colour scorched her cheeks as she realised that his eyes were still burning on her half-naked body. He was breathing hard and unevenly, as though he had been running for miles.

'Lee . . .?' Her uncertainty was in her voice, her hectically-flushed cheeks and shadowed eyes.

'Oh, Marie-Claire,' he said softly, reaching for her, lifting her to her feet, sliding the straps of her dress gently back on to her shoulders with hands that were slightly unsteady. 'God, you don't know how much I want you!' His voice was deep, liquid.

She lowered her dark head. 'Then why——?' She couldn't say it.

Lee sighed, his mouth twisting wryly. 'For your sake, you must believe that. God knows, all I want to do now is carry you to my bed—I want you so much, it's a gut pain.'

'Lee——' She responded to the rough violence in his voice, ready, so willing to give him anything he wanted. He couldn't want her more than she wanted him. That was an impossibility.

'No.' The word was dragged from his throat. 'I'm taking you back to your room—now—before I do something we'll both regret.' He bent his head and bruisingly kissed her mouth.

Marie-Claire closed her eyes, the touch of his mouth branding her for ever, and allowed him to lead her to the lift.

Outside Ran's suite, he smiled, though his face was tense, and bade her goodnight.

Dazed and still aching with desire, she reached up and touched his tanned face. Lee caught her hand, kissing her fingers before turning away and striding quickly towards the lift.

Alone, the shattering knowledge came to her that she was on the brink of falling in love with him, deeply and irrevocably in love with him. No, she thought fiercely, no, that's not the way I want it. I want some control in this affair. I won't be hurt again.

CHAPTER FOUR

THE following week passed so quickly it was like a hazy, half-remembered dream.

Marie-Claire spent most of her time with Lee—he jealously guarded her every available waking moment—and the rest of it with Ran, who seemed to be getting more and more involved with Bettina.

On Christmas Day, Lee took her out to lunch, and over the meal handed her a small brightly-wrapped box.

'Happy Christmas,' he said wryly, though his expression was gentle.

She took the box, wide-eyed. 'Oh, but I didn't get you a present!' she exclaimed in dismay.

Lee smiled. 'I'll think of something,' he promised, his eyes darkening as he looked at her.

Inside the padded, velvet-covered box lay a fine gold necklace studded with fiery rubies. It was old and delicate and very beautiful, obviously something special.

Marie-Claire's eyes filled with tears as she stared at it. 'Oh, Lee, it's so lovely, but I couldn't possibly accept it—I couldn't.'

Lee firmly overrode all her objections until she was forced to accept it, the only alternative being to insult him by refusing.

Over the days that followed she began to know him better. He was strong and gentle, honest, with a charm that took her breath away. He was witty, his mind brilliant, and his powerful male sexuality left her reeling.

She was in no doubt that he desired her fiercely, it was something he could not disguise, and she was also in no doubt that his need for her was reciprocated within herself. But when they kissed, when they touched, it was always Lee who drew back as though he was waiting for something. It was something Marie-Claire could not understand, and she lay alone in her vast bed every night, physically aching for him.

Two days after Christmas, Lee took her up to Gornergrat on the cogwheel railway. It was a journey she was to remember for the rest of her life.

The day was fine, the sky a pure unclouded blue as they walked hand in hand to the station. The long station building was full of brightly-dressed skiers crammed into the squares of wooden benches.

Lee bought their tickets from a guard smoking a crooked cigar who smiled broadly at Marie-Claire, then they sat on benches by the huge glass doors which slid open when the train arrived. The carriage was warm and full, and they sat by the pull-down windows on slatted wooden seats and began their forty-minute journey into the mountains.

Marie-Claire stared out of the windows entranced, as they left Zermatt behind on their slow ascent, watching the skiers shooting down the slopes they were climbing. Up and up they travelled, through stone tunnels cut through the mountains, the town below getting smaller and smaller until it was lost to view. The train stopped at Riffelberg, where there was a huge hotel that looked as though it was perched on the very edge of a precipice, then continued its slow climb to Gornergrat, over ten thousand feet above sea level.

Once through the ticket box, they climbed the snowy hill to the viewing platform, and the wind suddenly rose, whipping the powdery snow from the ground into their faces.

For a moment Marie-Claire couldn't breathe, and panic rose inside her. She couldn't get the air into her lungs, she couldn't see. She was going to die, she thought wildly. But Lee pulled her against his body, shielding her until the wind died down again. It passed in moments, but she pressed herself against him, her face buried against his chest, and felt frightened.

At the top of the hill stood a huge stone building with two golden-domed towers, and a tiny church. They walked up the steps together and stood on the observation terrace, Lee's arm around her shoulders.

Before them was the most spectacular view Marie-Claire had ever seen in her life; steep ravines, white mountains touching the sky, misty glaciers—a vast panorama as far as the eye could see. Huge black birds swooped below them, their wings fluttering against the white brilliance.

Marie-Claire held her breath, forgetting everything but what she saw around her. It was difficult to appreciate the sheer size, the sheer magnificence of the view, but its bleak, total hostility made her shiver. It would be so easy to die out here; who could have strength against such emptiness, such blindingly white loneliness? In these mountains, human life meant nothing, it was puny and weak compared to the elemental strength she saw around her.

She turned to Lee, resting her head against his hard shoulder, needing the reassurance of his closeness. She felt deeply aware of her own insignificance in the plan of things. She felt as though she was on the verge of understanding something fundamental about her life, but not quite able to reach out and find it.

She did realise one thing, though, and that was that life had to be lived to the full. She had to reach out and grab everything she wanted. She looked at the mountains and knew that she didn't have a moment to throw away or waste. Life was too short.

Later, she couldn't remember how long they stood there, but somehow the stark wintry mountains changed her, reaching some deep untouched part of her. She stared and stared at the mountains, at the birds, at the racing clouds, and held on to Lee very tightly. She looked up into his face and could read nothing at all, until their eyes met and he bent his dark head and kissed her mouth.

They ate lunch in the domed restaurant. Back to normality, Marie-Claire thought ruefully, watching the tourists laden with cameras. It was an old building with high stone walls and the atmosphere of an old draughty castle. It was incredible that it had ever been built in such a remote inaccessible place, she marvelled, as she sipped her hot rich coffee.

Outside again, as they waited for the train, Lee held her tightly, aware of the sweet melancholy of her mood, and told her the names of the mountains, old names that sounded like magicians' spells—Gabelhorn, Lyskamm, Stockhorn, Monte Rosa. Below, the skiers plunged down the almost-vertical snowy slopes, hardly noticing the beauty around them, and Marie-Claire felt her eyes filling with cold tears.

Lee sighed, his expression gentle as he wiped the tears away, swinging her into his arms and holding her very tightly.

'It's so beautiful, it hurts,' she whispered against his tanned cheek.

Lee smiled. 'I know,' he said softly. 'A view like this could drive a man insane. Our minds are too small to fully comprehend it.'

She nodded, knowing what he meant. And in the fading light as the train crawled slowly back down to Zermatt, she stared into his face, so glad that she had shared such an earth-shattering experience with him. She wouldn't have wanted to go there with anybody else in the world.

That evening he took her to a tiny basement restaurant for fondue, a national dish. The restaurant was dark, lit by candles, as they descended the steps, furnished in dark carved wood with gruesome masks hanging on the walls. In one corner, an accordionist played, filling the room with music.

At a gingham-covered table they drank wine and ate the dry bitter slices of air-dried Valais meat, served with bread and butter, and talked.

'Tell me about him,' Lee said suddenly in a quiet voice.

'Who?' Marie-Claire smiled at him, genuinely bewildered.

'The man who hurt you,' he replied expressionlessly, his narrowed grey eyes holding hers.

'Chris? There's nothing to tell. We were engaged, I found him in bed with someone else.' She saw Lee's jaw tightening and said quickly, 'It wasn't his fault, it's just the way he is. I was the one at fault, I tried to pretend he was something other than what he really was. I hurt myself, do you see?'

Lee was silent, staring at her with an expressionless intensity, and she wondered why he had wanted to know.

Strangely, she could talk about it easily now. She hadn't even thought of Chris for a few days. Had she ever loved him? she wondered. Had she ever loved Chris, the real person? If she hadn't caught him making love to that other woman, would she really have married him, married her own illusion? How could she have been so wrong? It was the only question she could never answer, and it was frightening, because she knew that the deeply romantic streak in her still dictated her actions to a great degree.

She looked into Lee's hard-boned face and thought—what do I really know about him? Am I wrong about him too?

Any thought of Chris always brought back a terrible insecurity.

At that moment the fondue arrived at the table, creamy yellow in a dish over a tiny blue flame. The smell was mouthwatering. The waitress also brought a basket full of bread cubes and two long-handled forks.

Lee showed Marie-Claire how to spear a cube of bread and dip it into the bubbling fondue. She tasted it tentatively and found it delicious, tasting strongly of wine, becoming thicker as it got hotter.

'I don't know anything about you,' she said as she ate,

'What do you want to know?' Lee asked indulgently.

'Tell me about your life—right from the beginning. How old are you, for a start?' she asked guilelessly.

He laughed. 'Thirty-seven, and I was brought up in an orphanage. I never knew my father, and my mother died giving birth to my sister who, unfortunately, also died when she was two days old. There were no relations, so I was put into a home.' He spoke in a voice devoid of any emotion whatsoever. He might have been talking about someone else, a stranger, but Marie-Claire's heart clenched with pain for him.

'Oh, no,' she whispered, her horror shadowing her eyes. 'That's awful!'

Lee smiled lazily. 'No, it was a long time ago, it doesn't matter any more, in fact, it taught me a hell of a lot about the world, and I'm thankful for that.'

He didn't want sympathy, she saw as she watched him; it had never even occurred to him that he deserved sympathy. For him it was merely a fact of life.

'Go on,' she prompted with a sweet smile. 'What did you do when you left the orphanage?'

'I got a job as a crew member on a rich man's yacht and travelled the world with him. He was old and lonely and we got on well. He loaned me the money to set up my business—he died before I'd paid it all back.' Lee's voice was expressionless as he spoke of his life, but Marie-Claire read between the lines. He had made his millions the hard way. It was a storybook life, one that she found totally impossible to imagine.

He was tough, hard, successful and very clever. His character was forceful and very complex, tempered by that rare gentleness that belongs only to the truly strong. He was an enigma, and it was easy to see why women found him so devastatingly attractive.

'You're difficult to get to know,' she said slowly, talking half to herself.

Lee laughed, a low attractive growl of amusement. 'Maybe.' He shrugged his powerful shoulders as though it didn't matter at all. 'Do you want to get to know me, Marie-Claire?'

She flushed, unable to drag her eyes away from his. 'Yes,' she whispered honestly, unable to lie.

He smiled. 'That's good to know.'

She looked away then, her heart pounding, aware of the sudden tension between them.

The dessert was fresh fruit with kirsch, but Marie-Claire refused it because the fondue had been surprisingly filling, settling for coffee.

Lee made her laugh as they talked, deliberately charming her, perhaps trying to make her forget what he had told her. She stared into his grey eyes, dark in the candlelight, and felt as though she was drowning. His eyes caressed her, shadowed with laughter, with desire, but as she laughed and talked, she *was* thinking of what he had told her about himself, and she was wondering about his marriage.

He was divorced, Ran had said, and he had a daughter. She had so many questions about that, but she didn't dare to ask them.

He did not talk easily about himself. If he wanted her to know, he would tell her.

After the meal, Lee took her to an ice hockey game. It was the first she had ever been to, and she found it exhilarating. It was held in the open air; the rink was floodlit, and the game attracted hundreds of spectators.

It was fast—the fastest game she had ever seen, and very exciting. It was difficult to believe that anyone could skate so fast, and it was fun standing in the crowd with Lee's arm around her, the scent of French cigarettes filling her nostrils, the outraged and ecstatic cries of the supporters filling her ears.

They ended up in a warm noisy bar drinking German beer, and Marie-Claire found herself—without realising it—revealing all her secrets to Lee, all her dreams, all the important things in her life. He listened carefully, never taking his eyes off her, even though she was certain that he couldn't find such a dull topic of conversation very interesting.

Back at the hotel, when she thanked him for a wonderful day, he took her into his arms, his mouth parting hers with a deep hunger. She clung to him, stroking her hands through the dark vitality of his hair, her mind and body accepting the fact that she had been waiting for this moment all evening, matching his hunger with a need of her own.

But again he drew back, kissing her eyelids, her cheeks, smiling down at her though his body was taut with desire.

And she lay alone again in her bed that night, twisting and turning against the cool sheets, aching for his possession.

Before she realised, it was New Year's Eve—a big event in the town, Ran told her, the festival of St Sylvester. Everywhere she looked she saw posters advertising dances, gala dinners, New Year balls and discos, and the excitement was almost tangible.

The hotel was holding a gala dinner-dance and Lee asked her to go with him. Marie-Claire happily agreed, knowing that Ran and Bettina as well as Rima and James would be there.

She asked Ran about Bettina that morning, over an early breakfast in his suite.

'What are your plans for today?' Ran asked casually, his mind half on something else.

She looked up from the newspaper she was reading and shrugged. 'Lee has promised to give me another skiing lesson, but he has some business to attend to this afternoon, so I haven't any particular plans.'

Worried that she was keeping him from the slopes, when she knew that he was a keen skier, Marie-Claire had urged Lee to go skiing. Smiling, he had offered to teach her instead, and she was getting on quite well, although she still felt frightened rather than exhilarated. Lee was a good teacher, patient and thorough, and she was enjoying it immensely.

'What about you?' she asked. 'Are you working?'

Ran nodded. 'I'll be working this afternoon, but I have a lunch date with Bettina.'

'Ah!' Marie-Claire pronounced, her eyes sparkling. 'Bettina.'

Surprisingly, Ran almost flushed, lowering his dark head.

'What's going on with you two?' Marie-Claire probed, mad with curiosity.

'The usual thing,' Ran replied with a smile, but his blue eyes told her that it was probably serious.

'Good, it's just what you need,' she told him, meaning every word. If it helped him to forget the woman he had fallen in love with the previous year, if he could fall in love with someone kind and pretty and bright like Bettina, she knew he would be happy.

'Isn't it just what everybody needs?' Ran replied, a faint bitterness in his voice that told her he wasn't quite over the other woman yet.

Late in the afternoon, Marie-Claire rang Becky in London. She wanted to hear her friend's news and she wanted to wish her a happy New Year.

Becky sounded glad to hear from her, telling her all the latest news, the latest gossip about their mutual friends, chattering on about the new play she was working on. Then she casually said something that jerked Marie-Claire up in her seat.

'*What* did you say?' she asked, her eyes widening.

'I said, we all went to Chris's reception on Saturday. . . .' Becky's voice trailed off in horror. 'Oh, no!' she moaned, utterly miserable. 'You didn't know, did you?'

Marie-Claire swallowed almost nervously. 'I don't know anything. What's happened? What reception?' She heard Becky sigh.

'I'm sorry, Marie-Claire, you know what I'm like— my mouth always runs away with me——'

'Tell me,' Marie-Claire cut in urgently.

Becky sounded embarrassed as she revealed quietly, 'Well, you're bound to find out sooner or later, I suppose—Chris got married on Saturday.' It was a totally unexpected bombshell.

'Married?' Marie-Claire echoed weakly. 'Anyone
. . . anyone we know?'

'I don't know her. Apparently her name is
Charlotte, and she looked about six months pregnant. . . .' Becky's voice trailed off again, as though she
knew she had made yet another ghastly mistake.

Six months pregnant—a woman he had obviously
been seeing while engaged to herself, Marie-Claire
thought bitterly. 'If you see him, give him my best
wishes, will you?' she said in a hard little voice.

'Yes, yes, of course.' Becky was still embarrassed,
and the conversation became so awkward that it was a
relief to finish talking and put down the receiver.

Marie-Claire sat on the bed, and suddenly realised
that she was crying. Chris's deceit still had the power to
hurt her. He had been a part of her life for a long time
and it wasn't easy to pretend that he had never existed.

By the time she dressed for dinner, she had
hardened herself to the news, a brittle calm masking
her hurt insecurity.

She had chosen her dress the day before; thin green
silk covered with tiny gold stars, it was full-skirted
and fashionable, leaving her pale shoulders bare. She
made up her face with tightly-controlled fingers, and
fastened the necklace Lee had given her around her
neck, then stepped into high-heeled shoes and brushed
her hair again.

Absently, she stood in front of the large mirror,
staring at her reflection with blind eyes. She looked
good, she knew without any particular pleasure. The
dress suited her perfectly, it enhanced the translucent
paleness of her skin and emphasised the curved shape
of her body.

Looking at the clock, she saw that she was ready too
early. A grim smile touched her lips. She was never
ready early!

She opened one of the windows and sat down, not even noticing the cold draught of air. She lit a cigarette, drawing on it deeply, though she rarely smoked, and stared out to where the mountains met the sky. Deep inside her there was a tight, cold knot of confusion that she couldn't dissolve or work out. There was a blankness in her mind that refused to allow her to think logically.

She didn't love Chris, she thought tiredly, it was nothing to do with Chris really, it was to do with her.

Lee's hard dark face rose before her eyes. She was already deeply involved with him, too desperately fighting a love that was becoming increasingly hard to deny herself. And yet in the back of her mind, she couldn't let herself trust him.

Why did he want her? She was nothing special, Chris had taught her that—and Lee had his choice of any beautiful women in the world. Why was he spending his time with her? She could think of no good reason, not a single one.

She couldn't let go of her mistrust, however hard she tried. She had been hurt once, and she knew instinctively that her pain over Chris was nothing to the heartbreak Lee could cause her. Lee could destroy her because her feelings for him were so strong now, so deep. So much for her ideas of controlling her own life, of taking what she wanted!

What could she do? There didn't seem much choice, she would be hurt either way.

'Oh, God,' she whispered aloud, 'I'm so unsure of myself, and of him. What can I do? What the hell can I do?'

The vast panelled dining room was richly decorated with golden streamers and balloons, the atmosphere bright and festive.

By each place setting stood a tiny model of a

chimney sweep—a symbol of good luck for every guest.

And there was music, and dancing, a jazz band playing happy music. But none of the festivity or the excited, frantically happy atmosphere could lift Marie-Claire's strange sadness.

'What is it?' Lee asked quietly, his grey eyes searching her face.

'Nothing,' she lied, lowering her head. 'New Year always makes me feel sad.' That at least was true, although she had never known why.

She sipped her wine too quickly, knowing the momentary urge to get good and drunk. At least that would block out her stupid aching misery.

Lee reached out, tilting up her chin with his thumb, forcing her to meet his cool probing gaze. Unable to look away, she stared at him, her eyes dark with sadness, filling with diamond tears.

'Dance with me.' He led her on to the dance floor and she was too surprised to object. As he took her into his arms, she felt his strength giving her back some life.

'Now, tell me,' he commanded, his mouth against her silky hair.

'I'm frightened,' she admitted huskily, letting her fingers splay against the hard muscles of his shoulders.

'Of what, Marie-Claire?'

'I don't know.' She couldn't tell him the whole truth, she didn't even know it herself. 'Lee, can we go outside for the New Year?' Suddenly she needed some air, and she needed to be alone with him.

'Sure.' He smiled down at her, and her heart turned over.

And as he promised, they left the hotel after eleven. The streets were crowded and noisy. She allowed him to take her hand as they walked towards the fountain

in the centre of the town. People passed them holding
candles, people in fancy dress with painted faces. The
atmosphere was that of a carnival. There was a big
crowd gathered in the square near the fountain, and as
church bells began to echo all over the valley, the New
Year was born.

Suddenly the sky was filled with exploding
fireworks and flares, people were cheering and
dancing, and from a nearby restaurant came the sound
of crashing cymbals and voices singing.

Marie-Claire, strangely vulnerable, open to the
ecstatic celebration around them, felt the tears pouring
uncontrollably down her face.

Lee took one look at her and lifted her into his arms,
holding her so tightly that her feet weren't touching
the ground. He kissed her cheeks, then parted her lips
with his own in a deep drugging kiss that had her
clinging to him in seconds.

She laughed, rather hysterically, and flung her arms
around his neck, and when he lifted his dark head she
smiled into his shadowed grey eyes.

'Happy New Year,' he said softly, smiling back at
her.

'Happy New Year to you,' she replied gravely, her
small face still wet with tears.

'Marie-Claire, why are you crying?' There was a
wry gentle indulgence in his voice as he kissed away
the tears, and the clean warmth of his breath against
her face made her tremble.

'I thought I was sad, but maybe I'm happy after all.'
Her mood was as quick as lightning, confusing her as
she replied.

The bells were still ringing as they walked back
through the crowded streets. People sprinkled them
with glitter and confetti, shouting greetings and best
wishes. It was like a huge, open-air masquerade.

In the deserted hotel foyer, Lee helped her out of her coat.

'I don't want to go back in there,' she said quickly, before her courage failed her. 'Can we go to your suite?'

Lee nodded silently and led her into the lift.

The lights were dimmed in the huge lounge, and Marie-Claire wandered over to the windows, staring out at a sky still exploding with fireworks.

'Do you want a drink?' Lee's low voice raised the hair on the back of her neck.

'A glass of wine, please.' She sounded breathless and her heart was beating very fast in her ears. She turned and looked at him, her mouth drying, her throat aching with tension, as he came towards her, a tall dark powerful man with grey eyes that turned her knees to water.

As he handed her the glass of wine, Marie-Claire made her decision. She wanted him, wanted him so much it was a fever inside her. She wanted to spend the night in his bed, in his arms.

She drank her wine quickly, watching him throw back his scotch, watching the warm masculine line of his mouth, aching to feel it against her skin. She wanted to touch his powerful male body, she wanted him to make love to her.

She walked over to him on legs that trembled violently. Their eyes met and the tension between them was suddenly electrifying.

'Marie-Claire——' His voice was low, husky.

'I want you, Lee. Don't send me away tonight,' she pleaded softly, reaching up to touch the hard bones of his face.

His eyes darkened, lingering on the inviting softness of her mouth.

'You don't know what you're saying,' he said

harshly, his breath coming unevenly. 'Marie-Claire, you'd better get the hell out of here now, because if I touch you, God help me, I won't be able to let you go!'

Her answering smile was pure and beautiful, trapping the breath in his lungs, and she stood on her toes and kissed his mouth.

'I want you to touch me, I want you to hold me,' she whispered against his lips. 'Take me to bed.'

She heard him groan as her body was crushed against his, those powerful arms holding her tightly as his mouth parted hers, showing her his raw hunger and an aching need that made her shudder, clinging to him as the world rocked crazily beneath her feet. His mouth moved endlessly on hers, drugging her with passion and arousing in her a desire that beat like flame through her body, until her blood was roaring in her ears, deafening her.

I love him, she finally acknowledged to herself. I'll always love him. She couldn't have come to him like this if she did not love him.

Lee's mouth was at her throat, his tongue flicking sensuously against her skin, against the pulse that thundered there.

'Lee——' she murmured his name, on a soft moan of pleasure, and he lifted his head, breathing raggedly, his eyes glittering fire.

'God, how I want you,' he muttered huskily. 'You've haunted me for five years, Marie-Claire, and now I'm almost afraid to touch you——'

She stopped him with her mouth giving him her answer, her love, her yielding body begging for his touch.

Lee lifted her into his strong arms and effortlessly carried her to his bed, where he laid her down on the silken coverlet and arched over her. She reached for him, moaning softly as he kissed her throat, his long fingers moving deftly, sliding away her clothes until she was naked beneath his seeking hands.

Then his mouth followed the path laid bare by his hands, grazing fire over her skin, his tongue teasing her swollen nipples, the vulnerable softness of her stomach, moving lower still, his hands gently parting her pale thighs.

He made love to her until she cried out, arching herself innocently against him, lost to the slowly-building intensity that was beating its path up through every nerve in her body. Her heart was beating so fast, she thought it would kill her.

Then Lee moved and the warm air of the room felt cool against her heated flesh. He was undressing, carelessly pulling the clothes from his body. And she watched, hardly able to breathe as she looked at him.

He was so big, so strong, powerful tanned shoulders, a hard muscular chest rough with fine dark hair that arrowed down past the muscular flatness of his stomach to lean hips and long hair-roughened legs.

Marie-Claire gazed achingly at his powerful male purity, the stark magnificence of his body. He reached for her again, his smouldering gaze blazing over her own aroused naked body.

'The light——' she whispered, her throat dry, her colour rising shyly as he stared down at her.

'I want to see you,' he answered raggedly. 'Dear God, you're so beautiful—I don't think a lifetime could ease this ache inside me——'

His mouth was against hers then, demanding, hungry, his possessive hands sweeping fiercely over the soft curves of her body, stroking, caressing her, arousing her so feverishly that she cried with pleasure.

'Touch me,' he groaned, placing her clenched hands against the damp hair of his skin. 'Make love to me.'

She obeyed eagerly, her hands shaping the tense muscles of his shoulders, stroking his smooth brown skin. Her mouth moved slowly over his chest, her nostrils filled with his cleanly erotic male scent, and she was aware of his heart pounding heavily as her tongue flicked against his hair-roughened skin.

He was beautiful, she thought achingly. Her hands moved lower, followed by her mouth, over his flat stomach. He was shaking, his powerful body racked by convulsive shudders, he was groaning hoarsely as she made love to him. To touch him so freely, so lovingly, was fiercely pleasurable, arousing her even more desperately, the feel of his skin sending electricity coursing through her.

Then, as though he could bear it no longer, Lee's hands closed over hers and he pulled her up against him, rolling so that she lay beneath him, his hard dominant body pinning her to the soft bed. His mouth touched hers again, his need like fire, his hands stroking over her, until she was writhing, begging for his possession.

The he took her, the smooth deep rhythm of his powerful body as he parted her thighs a thrusting strength that drove them both to the limit of fulfilment.

Marie-Claire was lost, clinging blindly to the sweat-dampened heat of Lee's body, her nails raking the smooth skin of his taut back, aware that his hands were still moving on her body. And when the climax came, and the unbearably intense spiral burst through every barrier into a shattering fulfilment, she heard her own sobbing cries of satisfaction, heard Lee's deep hoarse groaning, his fierce tension breaking, their bodies twisting together, burning up with heat.

Later, she lay moaning softly, the weight of Lee's body on top of her, his dark head bent to her breasts.

He was breathing as though he was dying, sucking the air into his lungs, his heart was hammering, matching hers beat for beat.

She closed her arms around him, so glad, so very glad that he had made love to her. He was her first lover, and his patient expertise had given her a shattering destroying pleasure, a fulfilment she could never have imagined.

I love you, she whispered silently, stroking his black hair, delighting in his responsive shudder as he kissed her breasts.

He moved then, lying on his side, resting his head on his hand to look down at her with dark sensual eyes. Marie-Claire lay on her back, her body still weak, still aching with pleasure, her shyness gone as she met his gaze.

Lee reached out his hand and tenderly traced the swollen line of her mouth. 'Marry me,' he said huskily.

Marie-Claire smiled lazily, gasping as his hand slid gently to her breasts, her body tautening again, aching, as her nipples hardened.

'Yes,' she agreed softly, her heart bursting with happiness. 'Ah, Lee——'

She turned to him in sudden need and he began to kiss her mouth.

CHAPTER FIVE

IT seemed, as Ran had said, that Lee was a very powerful man. Their marriage was arranged immediately in the English church, and everything was moving so fast that Marie-Claire barely had time to blink.

Ran, worried about the suddenness of it all, took one look at the love burning in her eyes, and wished her every happiness.

She was happier than she had ever been in her life before, and it showed for anyone with any doubts to see.

Rima was ecstatic when she heard. 'Oh, I'm so happy for you both!' she smiled as they drank coffee together in the hotel lounge.

'Thank you.' Rima's approval meant a lot to Marie-Claire.

The older woman smiled. 'I've known Lee for a long time now——' And when she saw Marie-Claire's curious glance, she explained, 'He and James have been friends for years—James used to work for Lee. Anyway, since the divorce—oh, I don't know, I suppose Lee was bitter—he had every right to be. He'll have told you about Naomi, of course——'

Lee hadn't. He had never mentioned her to Marie-Claire, but she could hardly tell Rima that, so she nodded as though she knew everything and let the other woman continue. 'She hurt him badly, although of course he never gave anything away. I know he's been lonely—he shut himself away, you know, after the divorce and that awful business over Laurie.'

Rima paused, sipping her coffee, and Marie-Claire had to stop herself asking the barrage of questions that were burning in her brain, hovering on her lips. She wanted to know about Naomi and Laurie, she wanted to know *everything*, but how could she ask Rima? Rima was a good friend, but she was Lee's friend too, and such confidences could be awkward for them both.

'I'm so glad it's you,' Rima continued, her eyes very bright. 'Lee's been so much more like his old self since you came here. He needs a woman of gentleness and compassion—someone who can heal the wounds Naomi left.'

Marie-Claire smiled in silence. He must have loved his wife very much, she thought, a dart of jealousy shooting through her, a dart of compassion for the pain he must have suffered. If she wanted to know all the details she would have to ask Lee, and she didn't know that she had the courage to do that just yet.

Two days later they flew back to England. On the plane, Marie-Claire rested her head against Lee's wide shoulder and slept. It was incredible how everything had happened so fast, the previous forty-eight hours had spun by like a speeded-up film. She was Lee's wife now, the heavy gold band on her wedding finger marking her as his possession.

It had been a quiet wedding, with only Ran and Bettina and Rima and James there. Marie-Claire had been a mass of nerves, breathtakingly beautiful in pure white embroidered silk. Lee's eyes had darkened with emotion as she came to him at the altar.

She had listened to his voice as he took the vows, deep and sure and firm, while her own had been high and breathless.

Somehow the news of their wedding had spread all over the town, and a huge unexpected reception had been organised for them. It had lasted until dawn the next day, although they had not stayed that long.

Lee's power in the town could not be doubted, Marie-Claire had thought, as the men respectfully congratulated them and the women openly assessed her—wondering, no doubt, how she had managed to capture the interest of a man like Lee Harper.

The night since their wedding had been spent passionately. Lee was an expert lover, hungry for her, and she wanted him badly, her own need matching his. And it was so wonderful to wake every morning in the strong circle of his arms. It completed her.

She sighed now as she gazed out of the tiny window on the plane, wondering at her suddenly melancholy mood. Everything was so perfect—could it really last? Could anything so perfect stand the test of time?

The plane was descending into the greyness of Gatwick airport. It was raining heavily, London looking bleaker than ever, and already Zermatt seemed years away, a dream that was still fresh in her memory.

Marie-Claire felt Lee's eyes on her and turned to him. He kissed her, his firm mouth brushing hers. 'Why so sad?'

She shrugged, her black hair swinging around her delicate face. 'Coming home, I suppose, and . . . and I'm a little nervous about meeting Laurie.' It had been a joint decision that they came back to England, postponing their honeymoon for a few weeks so that Marie-Claire could get to know Lee's daughter.

Lee touched her face. 'There's nothing to be nervous about—she'll love you, I promise.' There was a calm certainty in his voice that allayed her fears and gave her confidence.

Yes, she *would* make Laurie like her, she thought fiercely. Everything *would* be all right.

But as they drove out of London in Lee's low black

car, that feeling of foreboding that had been hovering over her all day refused to be pushed away, frightening because she could find no reason for it.

Lee's house was in the country, although within easy commuting distance of London. A few miles outside a time-untouched village, high wrought iron gates marked a gravel drive, down which the car shot smoothly to pull to a halt outside the front porch of an enormous white stone house, half covered with climbing ivy.

Marie-Claire fell in love with it on sight, gasping with delight as she stepped out of the car.

'It's beautiful,' she murmured, smiling at him.

Lee took her arm and led her up the old stone steps and inside into a warm mahogany-panelled hall where bowls of fresh flowers scented the air and welcomed them both.

After a quick cup of coffee, at Marie-Claire's excited insistence, they spent the next half hour exploring the house. Lee showed her every room—so many that her head was spinning—and explained about his house-keeper, Mrs Ingram, who attended to all domestic matters, and whom Marie-Claire would meet the following day.

Then at last they were in Lee's bedroom, a vast room decorated with flair in deep greys and rich blues. She wanderd around the room staring out of the long windows, at the trees and the wild gardens, her feet sinking into the thick Persian carpets. There were polished wood fittings and the bed was huge, covered in deep blue silk.

She turned to Lee, about to compliment him on his perfect taste, and found him staring at her with dark narrowed eyes. The words died in her throat as their glances locked, an aching tension winding around them, isolating them in a sweet web of desire.

'Marie-Claire——' He was at her side in a second, reaching for her, his lean hands sliding around her body to pull her closer. His mouth touched hers with deep hungry need.

They made love fiercely, a white-hot desire burning between them, twisting them together in restless desperation, Lee's hands almost violent as they swept over her body, until the final moments when Marie-Claire clung to him as though she was drowning, her body ripped apart by sensation.

Later, they showered together, laughing like children in the huge luxurious marble bathroom, and as Marie-Claire dressed in jeans and a black cashmere sweater, the telephone rang.

'Shall I answer it?' she called to Lee.

His deep amused voice came back. 'Sure—you live here now, remember?'

Laughing, she picked up the receiver. 'Hello?'

There was silence at the other end for a moment, a hesitation, then a soft husky woman's voice said. 'Put Lee on, would you, darling?'

Marie-Claire placed the receiver carefully near the telephone, the strange foreboding that had been threatening to consume her all day prickling down her spine now. She walked into the dressing room where Lee was reaching for a dark shirt, his powerful shoulders gleaming in the afternoon light.

'It's for you,' she said quietly.

He swore under his breath. 'Who is it?'

'I don't know.' Her glance rested hungrily on the play of muscles under his tanned skin as he pulled on the shirt.

He strode over to the telephone. 'Yes?' he demanded impatiently. 'Naomi, what the hell do you want?'

Hearing his ex-wife's name, Marie-Claire quickly

left the room, running down the polished oak staircase into the lounge. She stood by the long windows staring out at the misty lawns, her heart suddenly aching for something she did not understand.

Lee found her as he walked silently into the room, minutes later. He stared at her, so dark and beautiful, her face pressed against the glass, a graceful sadness in the droop of her slim shoulders.

'That was Naomi,' he told her expressionlessly.

Marie-Claire nodded, not turning to look at him. She knew.

'I have to drive up to London.'

She looked at him then, but his face was unreadable. 'Oh.' She didn't question him; she was afraid of what he might tell her if she did. Naomi's soft beautiful voice rang in her ears. The woman who owned that voice would be beautiful too, beautiful, confident, special—everything I'm not, Marie-Claire thought ruefully.

Lee came towards her, gently placing his hands on her shoulders. 'She's flying to Paris this evening, she wants me to pick Laurie up now.' His voice was cynical, harsh and his mouth was tight.

'Of course.' Marie-Claire tried to smile, not really understanding why he was so furiously angry.

'I'll be back as soon as I can.' He half-smiled at her, then bent his head, parting her lips in a fierce passionate kiss. Her arms crept around his neck, fingers eagerly stroking the thick vital hair as she returned his passion. And when he reluctantly raised his head, his eyes were shadowed with emotion. He didn't let her go but held her with possessive hands.

'Dammit, I'm sorry, Marie-Claire. I didn't expect this, I thought you'd have a chance to settle in before Laurie arrived,' he said softly.

'It doesn't matter,' she smiled at him. 'Actually, I'm

looking forward to meeting her. Shall I make a meal, or do you think——?' She broke off. She was anxious to start off on the right foot with Lee's daughter, but she shouldn't fuss.

He kissed her forehead. 'Would you mind? I was going to take you out tonight, but now that probably isn't such a good idea.'

'I'll cook something,' she promised, kissing him.

Then he was gone. She listened to the powerful roar of the car engine as it shot down the drive, and then she was alone in the big beautiful house.

She walked through all the rooms again, slowly this time, taking everything in. The house was beautifully decorated, furnished with a mixture of antique and modern furniture, full of books and paintings, records and tapes.

She made the bed, the disorderly sheets witness to the fierce passion she and Lee had shared. She already loved this house. It had welcomed her the moment she stepped inside the front door.

Back in the lounge again, she looked at the carved mantelpiece surrounding a tiled grate and decided to light a fire, not because it was cold—the central heating was excellent—but because she loved real fires and she wanted to make everything as nice as possible for Laurie's return.

She was longing to meet Lee's daughter, yet she was terribly nervous. What if the child hated her? What if they couldn't get on at all?

Lee had not said much about his daughter, apart from the fact that she was a normal healthy six-year-old, bright and intelligent, but not, he feared, happy enough.

Wait and see, Marie-Claire told herself as she piled logs into the grate. There was no point in working herself up into a nervous panic before the little girl arrived.

She lit the fire without difficulty and sat back on her heels, pushing her hair out of her face and unknowingly streaking her cheeks with soot. She stared into the struggling flames and wondered about her mood today. Perhaps it was just nerves. And the fact that she would now be meeting Laurie had not eased any of her tension. First impressions were so important—especially with children. Should she change? She stared down at her tight jeans and loose black jumper and smiled ruefully. There she went again, panicking! She had to pull herself together and relax.

'There you are, darling.' The low, amused woman's voice behind her jerked round her head and she found herself looking at a stunning auburn-haired beauty, who was watching her with coolly amused eyes.

Marie-Claire got to her feet, aware by that amusement that she probably looked a sight. 'Hello,' she managed as calmly as she could. 'Who are you?'

'Melissa Sinclair,' the woman revealed, still staring, quickly assessing Marie-Claire's slender graceful body, her youth, her beauty.

She was very pretty, Marie-Claire thought inconsequentially, although the woman's name certainly didn't ring a bell and didn't answer her question.

'I'm Marie-Claire Harper,' she offered with a smile.

'I know—Lee's new little wife,' said Melissa Sinclair, her eyes suddenly hard. 'I take it Lee's not in?'

Marie-Claire frowned. 'No, he had to go out.' How on earth had this woman got into the house? She obviously knew Lee. 'Can I get you some coffee?' she asked politely.

Melissa Sinclair nodded. 'Yes, we can have a chat. You'll excuse my just dropping in, but the back door was open——' Her voice wasn't at all friendly underneath the charm.

Half sighing to herself, Marie-Claire led the way into the large light kitchen and switched on the coffee percolator, wishing that Lee was there. She sensed malice in Melissa Sinclair and she wasn't in the mood for fighting.

She eyed the other woman covertly as she searched the cupboards for cups. Melissa Sinclair was lounging gracefully against the tall fridge, wearing tight designer jeans and a beautifully-cut jacket over a silky hand-knitted sweater. Her make-up was perfect, her hair wild—a picture of studied carelessness, carelessness that is only achieved expensively.

Marie-Claire knew before she asked that Melissa Sinclair didn't take sugar in her coffee, and as they sat down at the polished kitchen table, Marie-Claire felt the nerves in her stomach tightening.

'Do you live near here, Miss Sinclair?' she asked politely, trying for a bit of pleasant conversation.

'Yes, just the other side of the village,' the woman replied in a bored voice. 'When were you married?'

Surprised by the sudden question, Marie-Claire stammered, 'Two days ago . . . why?'

Melissa Sinclair shrugged her slim shoulders. 'Yes, you still have that——' she paused'—untouched look about you.' She made it sound as though it was something vaguely distasteful.

Marie-Claire half-smiled. Was she supposed to answer that?

'You're a friend of Lee's?' she asked calmly.

'Oh, yes.' Melissa Sinclair's smile was satisfied, secretive.

Marie-Claire felt her stomach turning over. She had the feeling that she had fallen right into the other woman's trap. What was she saying?

'We're very close friends—all three of us, really. Lee, Naomi and myself, although I have to look after number one where Lee is concerned—every girl for herself, if you know what I mean.'

The message was deliberately callous and more than clear, and Marie-Claire paled, although she was determined not to show a single thing to Melissa Sinclair.

'Really?' she said coolly, unable to touch her coffee now. 'A pity for you, then, that he's married me.'

Melissa's opaque eyes glinted with anger as Marie-Claire's words hit home, but she only said coldly, 'Not particularly, especially when you consider that we all know *why* Lee married you.'

'We?' Marie-Claire queried, her voice shaking a little.

'Naomi and myself,' Melissa furnished with a smug smile.

'I think you'd better leave,' said Marie-Claire, getting to her feet. This woman was poisonous, and she didn't have the strength to fight. Her nerves were stretched like wire, a terrible uncertainty seeping insidiously through her mind. She's lying, she thought to herself. She's cold and malicious and she wants to cause trouble.

But why should she lie? Because she was Naomi's friend? Because she wanted Lee for herself?

Surely she can see that I'm no competition, that I have no weapons against her, Marie-Claire thought in confusion, this confrontation surprising her. 'I'll tell Lee that you called,' she added, her eyes blank, her voice cold.

Melissa Sinclair obviously wasn't used to being thrown out, and her beautifully-painted mouth tightened as she rose indolently to her feet, a hard spite gleaming in her eyes. 'You'd better,' she retorted smoothly, the implication being that Lee would not take kindly to hearing that Marie-Claire had practically thrown her out of the house. 'Oh yes, you've won today, darling—I'm going. You're arrogant now, but it won't last, and the sooner you realise why Lee married you the sooner you'll realise that you've made a big mistake.'

The way she spoke made Marie-Claire tremble inside. She was sick of Melissa's fencing.

'Very well, as you're obviously dying to, why don't you tell me why Lee married me?' It was a mistake to ask, she knew that as soon as the words were spoken. It revealed her nagging insecurity to the clever, spiteful woman in front of her. It gave Melissa another chance to wound her.

'My pleasure. I'll spell it out, shall I?' The question was rhetorical, Marie-Claire assumed, and didn't even bother to look up. 'Naomi is about to take Lee to court to try and revoke the judge's custody ruling that Laurie lives with him. He needs a wife, a stable family background, to convince the judge that he's still a fit father, that he can still offer Laurie everything she needs.' Melissa smiled at the pale horror in Marie-Claire's eyes, a horror that the younger girl was desperately trying to hide.

'If that's the case,' Marie-Claire said weakly, 'how come you didn't offer yourself as candidate for Lee's wife?'

Melissa smiled again, shocking Marie-Claire anew as she revealed, 'I'm already married, darling. This farce of a marriage nicely covers that up as well, should there be any investigation into Lee's—affairs.' She laughed. 'He's brilliant! Oh, I can see why he chose you, so naïve, so innocent, you're already in love with him, aren't you, you little fool.'

She moved towards the back door, her expensive French perfume filling the room, making Marie-Claire feel sick, and left the house without another word, without a backward glance.

'I don't believe you!' Marie-Claire almost shouted at the closed door. 'You're lying, *lying!*'

She sank down on to a chair, her stomach churning as she lit a cigarette. She didn't want to believe a word Melissa had said, but her mind wouldn't rest, wouldn't stop going over and over what the other woman had revealed.

Lee needed a wife if he was to keep Laurie. He couldn't, he *wouldn't*, she thought fiercely. But clever bitchy Melissa had sown a tiny seed of doubt in a mind that was still unsure of itself, and of the world, a heart that still found it difficult to trust even those it loved.

There was more reason for Lee to lie than Melissa, she thought wildly. Lee had more to gain, while Melissa, if she was to be believed, already had what she wanted.

As darkness fell, Marie-Claire sat alone in the kitchen, the meal forgotten, desperately needing reassurance and receiving none. It seemed as though Lee had been gone for hours and hours. Chris's deceit had scarred her deeply, and without someone to talk logically to her, her irrational mind ran riot.

What if she had made the same mistake again? Implicitly trusting someone when there was no basis for that trust? How could she trust Lee? She had known him for such a short time. Hadn't her every contact with men shown her how deceitful they were, how they used people only for their own ends?

Lee's lean dark face rose before her eyes. He was a hard man. He knew what he wanted and he took it. He faced the world alone and forced it to give in. He desired her, but he had never told her that he loved her, not once, she realised with dawning dismay. Perhaps that desire was just a bonus in his plan of things. Perhaps——

'*Stop it!*' she told herself fiercely, speaking out loud. How could she be thinking like this? She loved him so deeply. A bitter smile touched her lips. That was the root of the problem. It would destroy her if she found out that he was only using her.

I'll ask him, she thought, desperately trying to pull herself together. I'll confront him with what Melissa Sinclair said.

She got shakily to her feet and walked into the dark lounge, her teeth chattering with sudden deathly cold. She switched on a lamp that bathed a circle of the carpet in soft intimate light, and sat down in front of the fire, curling herself up into a defensive ball, staring into the flames that could not warm her.

Would she have the courage to face Lee with her questions? Wouldn't the fear of what he might tell her keep her silent? Was it better to know and suffer the agony if Melissa was right? Could she bear to live without him if she had to leave?

The unanswerable questions kept coming, filling her head to bursting point. Desperately confused, she lit another cigarette. Half of her mind knew that her thoughts were wildly irrational, that she was deliberately persecuting herself, but she couldn't stop. She tried to think of Lee's face, the dark tenderness in his eyes when they made love, the smouldering intensity when he reached for her, the hunger of his mouth.

She only had to take one small step, she only had to trust him. He had, after all, never done anything to merit her distrust. He had always been gentle, kind, passionate—everything a lover could be.

Why, oh, why then couldn't she cross that thin line? Was she so weak, so frightened of being hurt again? It seemed she was, because that one step defeated her, leaving her totally isolated and alone, trembling with cowardice and indecision.

'Oh, God, help me,' she whispered, terribly weary.

At that moment the doorbell rang, breaking into her dreary thoughts with loud insistence. She got to her feet, moving slowly, her thoughts still running in frantic circles. On the doorstep stood the very last person she had expected to see: Chris. For a moment she just stared at him, shocked speechless.

He looked tired. Two months ago, sympathy would have clenched her heart, but now she felt nothing. Absolutely nothing. She only wished he hadn't come.

'Chris?' she said at last, when it became clear that he wasn't going to break the silence.

He was staring at her intently as though she was a blinding vision. 'Hello, Marie-Claire.' He sounded as tired as he looked. It was raining heavily, she realised, his fine blond hair was plastered to his head, the shoulders of his jacket soaking.

'What are you doing here?' she asked, still shocked. 'How did you know——?'

'Can I come in?' He cut across her, his voice weary.

She looked at him in silence for a moment. She didn't want him in the house. 'I don't think. . . .' she began, but he moved towards her and she involuntarily stepped back.

'Look, I'm going to catch pneumonia if I stand out in this rain for much longer.' He half-smiled, but his charm couldn't touch her, it left her totally cold. For the hundredth time she wished Lee was back.

'Chris——' Her voice was a plea for him to go away. She was thinking, why did I ever avoid him? I can look at him and I feel nothing at all, except perhaps a little sympathy. It was incredible, after all those agonising weeks she only felt sorry for him. There wasn't even any friendship left.

'Marie-Claire, I only want to talk—please let me in.'

He was almost begging, she realised in surprise. 'We

don't have anything to talk about,' she said with a puzzled frown.

'Marie-Claire!'

Defeated, she knew that he wasn't going to go away. 'Very well, but you can't stay long. I'm expecting Lee back at any minute.' She knew that she had given herself away when he smiled. Now he knew that she was alone.

She led him into the lounge, her hands curling nervously at her sides. Once near the fire she turned to him immediately without asking him to sit down, and said, 'Well, what is it you want to talk about?'

She wanted to get it over with. She wanted him to go.

Before he had a chance to answer, though, the telephone began to ring. Sighing, Marie-Claire walked over and picked up the receiver.

It was Becky, her voice urgent, worried. 'Marie-Claire? Look, I think I'd better warn you, Chris was round this afternoon. He wanted your address and I'm afraid I gave it to him. I suppose I wasn't thinking straight——'

'I know,' Marie-Claire cut in, her eyes on Chris. 'He's here now. I'll have to go, Becky, I'll ring you later, okay?'

As she replaced the receiver, she could still hear Becky's tiny voice apologising.

When she had telephoned Becky from Switzerland to tell her about the wedding, she had given her friend her new address and telephone number. It explained how Chris had found her, anyway.

Turning back to him, she found him smiling. 'Loyal Becky, ringing to warn you, eh?'

Marie-Claire ignored that. 'What do you want, Chris?' she asked again, her anxiety growing.

'Aren't you going to offer me a drink?' He shifted uncomfortably, shrugging out of his wet coat as she replied stiffly.

'No, I'm not.'

He smiled again. 'Well, I guess I deserve that.' He looked around the beautiful, dimly-lit room. 'Very cosy—it's a nice place you've got here. You've certainly landed on your feet!'

Marie-Claire was silent, realising with a sinking heart the intimacy of the situation, the one lamp enclosing them in a rosy romantic glow. If she switched on the rest of the lights, he would know how worried she was, he would press the advantage of his presence.

She would just have to pretend that she hadn't noticed how intimate the lighting was, that it didn't bother her one way or the other.

'I wish you would get to the point,' she said coolly, not looking at him.

'The point?' Chris laughed, but it was obvious that he was subdued. Once he had been exuberant, full of life, now he was quiet, broken somehow. That was why she felt sorry for him, Marie-Claire decided. 'There is no point, I just wanted to see you.'

She didn't know what to make of his words. She couldn't understand why he had come, no intention of and had encouraging him in any way at all.

'Well, now you have,' she told him quietly. 'I'm sure you understand—we only got back today and I'm rather busy, so if you'll excuse me. . . .' She allowed her voice to trail off, hoping he would take the hint. She didn't want to have to be rude to him, as she had been to Melissa Sinclair.

The thought of that woman brought all she had said back to Marie-Claire's mind, temporarily cleared by Chris's surprise appearance. And with the remembrance came a fresh wave of pain.

'Are you happy, Marie-Claire, with your new husband, your new life?' Chris asked suddenly, staring at her.

'Yes, I am—happier than I've ever been in my life,' she answered quietly, fighting down a wave of ridiculous hysteria. Happy? She was lying through her teeth. Two hours ago she had been happy, though, deliriously happy—too happy, probably. Why could she never remember that nothing lasted?

Chris's mouth twisted rather bitterly, but he said, 'I'm glad for you, and I'm sorry for what happened——'

'It's all in the past now,' Marie-Claire said quickly. If there was one thing she didn't want it was Chris to start dragging up old times. 'I think we should leave it there, don't you? Becky told me you were married—congratulations.' She was desperately trying to bring him back to the present, the future, to point out how their lives no longer had any point of contact. Go, she was willing him silently, just go, please!

'It's the worst mistake I've ever made in my life!' Chris burst out, suddenly surprising her. 'Marie-Claire, I——'

'Please, Chris, I really don't think that it's any of my business. I think you should go now, it would be the best thing.' She spoke quickly, masking her hesitancy, her shock at his admission.

He ignored her, and moved closer. 'You've got soot on your face,' he said quietly, putting a hand on her shoulder, raising the other one to gently wipe away the black smears from her cheek.

When she thought about it afterwards, Marie-Claire winced at how it must have looked, Chris holding her, his hand touching her face while she stood passive, unresisting, shocked that he dared.

But there was no going back, and as Chris murmured her name, the lounge door opened and in the doorway, staring at the scene before him with hard blank eyes, stood Lee.

CHAPTER SIX

Marie-Claire felt her heart lurching violently, a guilty colour pouring into her cheeks even though she had done nothing wrong.

Lee's body was very tense, his fists clenched at his sides, his mouth ominously tight. And his eyes held hers, mercilessly burning her with a bitter cynicism.

She felt Chris stiffen, his hands dropping from her, as he responded to the waves of violence emanating from Lee, a dark flush creeping along the lines of his cheekbones.

'So this is your new husband,' he said almost sneeringly, trying to save face as he looked at her.

She did not reply, did not look at him, her eyes wide and tinged with fear as she watched Lee, who had not moved a muscle, but as he heard Chris speak moved into the room with angry indolence, his eyes hardening into ice.

'Get out of here.' He spoke calmly, expressionlessly, but the threat was there, and Chris responded nervously.

'Now, wait a minute——' he began, but Marie-Claire could see that he was—what? Afraid of Lee? She couldn't blame him. She looked at her husband and her own skin prickled with fear.

Lee didn't give Chris a chance to finish speaking. 'Get out,' he repeated coldly. 'And in future you'll keep away from my wife, do you understand?'

Marie-Claire shuddered at the grimness in his voice, the terrible violent anger, and she watched Chris crumbling beneath that threat of violence, moving, backing away in sullen silence, not even looking at her as he shot away like a frightened rabbit. The front door slammed shut behind him.

Lee was staring at her, his glinting eyes skimming over her tense slender body, the guilty colour running beneath her skin, the fear in her eyes.

At least she had the grace to look guilty, he thought bitterly. Naomi had only ever laughed.

Marie-Claire knew that she was damning herself, she knew that she was innocent and she knew what Lee was thinking.

'It didn't take you long, did it?' he bit out harshly, the words flaying her cold skin. 'The minute my back was turned!'

'You . . . you don't understand,' she whispered, her mouth bone dry.

Lee smiled humourlessly, and she could see the tight control he was holding on himself.

'Oh, I understand, sweetheart—I've been there, too many times before,' he told her briskly. 'And I'm telling you now, if I ever find him in my house again, God help me, I'll kill him!'

The bitter threat frightened her, his furious anger frightened her, but the fact that he thought she and Chris had been . . . .

She turned away from the very idea in horror. That was the worst thing of all.

'You don't understand,' she said again. 'Chris came——'

'Ah yes,' Lee cut in icily. 'The ex-fiancé. Well, you can spare me the sordid details, I really don't want to know.'

His cold words hurt, cutting into her like sharp knives and with the pain came the anger of the misunderstood. Why should he be so angry? she wondered resentfully. She had done nothing wrong.

He was the one who couldn't be trusted, if Melissa Sinclair was to be believed.

'You want to believe the worst, don't you?' she burst out in painful retaliation, too hurt now to check her words.

If she thought Chris had hurt her, that had been nothing to the pain she was feeling now. 'You're not interested in the truth.'

Lee's eyes were as hard as stone. 'You're damn right I'm not, and I don't need it spelled out.' His mouth twisted. 'I saw enough—dimmed lights, roaring fire——' He was still very angry, but there was a note of cold intense weariness in his voice, as though the whole business was beginning to bore him.

He was looking at her with contempt, as though he hated her, she thought wildly, violent tears blocking her throat. How could he not know that it had all been for him, for his daughter?

'You bastard,' she whispered, destroyed by his hard implacable coldness.

Violence leapt in his eyes as her insult hit home. He moved towards her in quick silence, his hands clamping around her shoulders, his long fingers bruising her bones in a remorseless grip.

'You'll find out just how much of a bastard I can be, if I find you with him again,' he told her contemptuously, his cool breath fanning her cheek.

'I'll see Chris any time I want!' she retorted with shaky defiance. 'Who the hell do you think you are, anyway, telling me who I can and who I can't see?'

Lee's fingers tightened, making her gasp with pain. Their eyes met, hers fearful and defiant, his unfathomable, icy cold, and a fierce primeval tension shot between them like lightning, rawly electric and frightening in its intensity, its power.

'I'm your husband,' he said expressionlessly. 'You belong to me.'

'No, I belong to myself,' Marie-Claire replied shakily, his possessiveness making her heart pound with worry.

Lee stared at her, his cold grey eyes hypnotic. 'I should have remembered that a woman can't be trusted as far as you can throw her,' he said too softly.

'Why did you marry me, then?' she demanded, her mouth tight with pain.

'Why the hell do you think?' That awful tension still bound them destructively, yet Lee's anger seemed to have disappeared completely beneath an iron self-control. His face was a hard blank mask, his eyes totally unreadable. Only his violent grip on the soft skin of her shoulders revealed the intensity of his feelings, the effect of the terrible nerve-racking awareness between them.

Marie-Claire licked dry lips. Now was the time to confront him with what Melissa Sinclair had told her. Something shrank inside her at the thought of asking him, a pain twisting deep in her heart.

'A——' she paused, 'friend of yours called while you were out ... Melissa Sinclair.' She searched his blank eyes for some sort of reaction, but found none. He was silent and she was forced to continue haltingly, 'She told me that ... that your wife is contesting the custody ruling on Laurie.' Her voice trailed off. She suddenly felt so weak and so tired that she couldn't for the life of her frame the question she so desperately needed answering.

She stared into Lee's strong-boned face. Is that why you married me? her eyes asked in pleading silence. Is it? *Is it?*

Lee's fingers relaxed their bruising grip on her shoulders and he turned away from her so abruptly that she almost fell.

She watched the powerful line of his shoulders, the tanned strength of his hands as he lit a cigarette. He drew on it deeply, the pale smoke drifting from his lips as his eyes met hers again.

'What Melissa told you is the truth,' he said smoothly, almost indifferently, and Marie-Claire felt her heart clenching with agony, as his voice hardened. 'Believe me, Marie-Claire, I'll do anything and everything in my power to keep Laurie with me.'

It was the answer she had dreaded with every fibre of her being, and so casually brutal that she felt herself hit, exploding with white-hot anger, her only desire to hurt him as he had so callously hurt her.

'Do you know something, I wish I'd married Chris—I wish to God I'd married anybody but you!' she said fiercely, and knew a moment of triumph as his face hardened, closing as though she had struck him.

Lee swore violently, flinging his half-smoked cigarette into the flames of the fire, striding towards her with such menace that she backed away, trembling with fear, until she found herself trapped against the wall with no escape.

The atmosphere was explosive as he dragged her roughly against the hardness of his body, his hand tangling in her silken hair to pull back her head.

'It's too late for such regrets,' he said bitterly, his eyes glittering on the shaking line of her mouth. 'Much too late, Marie-Claire, because I'm not going to let you go—not now, not ever.'

His dark head was coming lower, the last words muttered against her skin as his mouth covered hers with a savagery that made her moan in protest.

She raised her hands, pushing futilely at the powerful unyielding muscles of his chest, her mind numb with pain. But Lee was much too strong for her, his mouth moving on hers with a brutal expertise that, somewhere inside her, ignited an unwilling answering hunger that took her by shameful surprise, beating up like an eagle's wings, so that in seconds her lips parted achingly beneath his. Her hands stopped fighting him, sliding up around his neck to hungrily stroke his black hair.

For a few moments Lee responded urgently to the passion overwhelming them, then suddenly his hands grasped her upper arms and he held her away from him, breathing heavily as he stared down at her soft inviting mouth, the drowsy responsive brilliance of her eyes.

His own eyes were shadowed, their expression veiled by narrowed lids. 'Goddammit, Marie-Claire,' he muttered harshly, and turning on his heel, strode from the room in silence.

Alone, Marie-Claire sank on to her knees in front of the fire, weakness flooding her. She felt the tears in her eyes, pouring freely down her hot cheeks now that he had gone.

They both knew that something had been broken between them, and that the damage was irreparable, that nothing would ever be the same again.

Was it only hours ago that they had made love so hungrily, with such passion, such need? It seemed like a million years ago. Lee had used her, she thought in defeat, used her as Chris had used her, and even when she had confronted him with what Melissa Sinclair had so eagerly revealed, he had shown no remorse.

He had not even tried to pretend that he had married her because he loved her. He had married her because he needed a wife to strengthen his position in court—he would do anything he had to, to keep his daughter with him.

She wiped away her tears with her fingers, a waste of time, as they seemed to be falling faster and faster.

How could she have been such a fool? How could she keep on making the same darned mistake? The questions echoed round and round in her empty mind. She had been blinded by desire, by love. Even now she had to acknowledge her love for him, a love she knew would never die.

Strangely, as she sat staring into the flames, and the moments ticked by, she began to feel calmer and she finally stopped crying.

For some reason, the knowledge that Lee couldn't kill her love for him gave her a crazy kind of strength. It was incredible and totally inexplicable but true, even though the pain inside her was an agony she could hardly bear. She had to leave, she couldn't stay here, she couldn't live with a man who didn't love her. Her heart winced as she thought of him, longed for him. Perhaps if she stayed he would come to care for her——

No, she would go tonight. She would go to London, to Becky, while she tried to pull herself together, pull herself out of this despairing pain.

She got to her feet, a curious numbness protecting her, and noticed as she looked at the clock that she had been sitting alone for over an hour.

The lights in the hall dazzled her sore eyes as she ran upstairs to wash her face. It was lucky that she hadn't unpacked, she could collect her things and be gone before Lee noticed.

She actually felt quite calm as she walked into the bedroom, although nothing could protect her from the pain searing her, as she looked at the huge bed where she had lain so passionately entwined with Lee only hours before.

On the point of entering the bathroom, she found her way suddenly blocked by him, his tanned skin gleaming wet as he stepped from the shower and wrapped a towel around his hips.

She faced him with a pounding heart, unable to stop herself staring at the powerful magnificence of his body.

'I . . . I'm sorry . . .' she stammered into the heavy silence, 'I didn't realise. . . .'

Lee raked a tense hand through his wet black hair, his narrowed eyes unreadable. Marie-Claire watched the tensing of the heavy muscles in his arms as though hypnotised.

'I've finished,' he said smoothly as he walked from the room, leaving her alone, to splash her face with icy cold water in an effort to reduce the swelling of her red eyes.

Back in the bedroom, she found Lee dressing, reaching for his shirt as she walked in.

'I'm leaving,' she told him quietly. 'I can't stay here.'

He stared at her, his blank grey eyes sliding over her tousled hair, the tear-washed paleness of her face and the rigid tension in her body.

'Oh, no,' he said very softly, very sure. 'I'm not going to let you walk out of here like this.'

Marie-Claire watched his hands as he buttoned the thin blue shirt, and her stomach trembled as she remembered those long lean fingers against her bare skin.

'You can't stop me,' she whispered painfully.

'I can, Marie-Claire, believe me,' he replied coolly, his eyes hard.

'Why should you want to?' she cried, shivering, her fragile reserves of calm crumbling before his cool certainty. 'We both know it was a mistake, we should never have got married—it . . . it was a mad, stupid impulse.'

Lee smiled, a twisting of his beautifully-moulded mouth, a smile that didn't touch the polished steel of his eyes.

'Is that what it was?' he queried expressionlessly. 'Poor Marie-Claire, all your love affairs disastrous—or has your ex-fiancé come up with an offer you can't refuse?'

The words were bitterly spoken and she flinched from them as though they were physical blows.

'Lee, please. . . .' She didn't know what she begged for, but she remained silent about Chris, biting back the denial that hovered on her tongue. If he thought her leaving had something to do with Chris, perhaps he would more easily let her go.

'Please?' he mocked softly. 'Please what, my love?'

He took a step towards her and she backed away in panic, her heart leaping into her throat as his wide shoulders blocked out the light.

'Lee, don't . . . please. . . .' She didn't look at him, her eyes fixed on the top button of his shirt, her attention caught for some crazy reason, by his smooth tanned skin beneath.

'You're trembling like a frightened child,' he mused softly, reaching out and tilting up her chin so that she was forced to meet the inscrutable grey depths of his eyes.

'You're my wife, Marie-Claire,' he told her in a harshly controlled voice, 'and I have no intention of letting you go. If I have to, I'll take you to bed now— I'll show you that you belong to me.' He saw the panic in her dark eyes and shook his head. 'Why are you so damned afraid of me?' he demanded tautly. 'A few hours ago——'

'I don't want to talk about it,' she cut in desperately. 'And if you need a woman so much, Melissa Sinclair made it patently clear that she would be more than willing to oblige——' she bit her lip savagely as she heard her own words. She sounded like a jealous wife! A bitter smile touched her mouth. Wasn't that just

what she was? She looked into the lean, achingly
familiar planes of Lee's face and realised with
incredulous wonder that she had already forgiven him
for his deceit, as she had never been able to forgive
Chris.

I love him so much, she thought fiercely, and
nothing else matters except that I'm here with him like
this.

'What the hell did she say to you?' Lee asked
curiously, still not releasing his hold on her, reading
her eyes, her expression.

Marie-Claire frowned. 'She . . . she told me about
the court case——' she revealed reluctantly.

'And?' Lee probed, knowing there was more.
Marie-Claire was silent, her eyes very dark, her mouth
very vulnerable. 'Tell me,' he persisted, but his voice
was suddenly gentle, which somehow hurt more than
his anger.

'She hinted that you and she are having an affair,'
she retorted honestly, stung into anger.

Lee half smiled and it was impossible to gauge his
reactions. 'And you believed her?'

She shrugged her slim shoulders. She had no
intention of answering that.

'It doesn't matter,' she lied huskily.

Lee released her chin, but still held her trapped
against the wall. 'You might as well know that I have
no intention of taking such a tolerant line with you,'
he told her with smooth coolness.

Marie-Claire chewed on her lower lip. 'You mean
Chris?'

Lee's eyes darkened. 'That's exactly who I mean.'

'Even if I love him?' she queried curiously.

'Do you love him, Marie-Claire?' he demanded,
staring down at her with eyes that seemed to probe
into her very soul.

'Lee——' She didn't know what to say. If she said no, he would know the truth, if she said yes she would be lying, and she couldn't lie to him about Chris.

He was so close that she could see the smooth texture of his skin, the thick darkness of his lashes. She was aching for him, she realised defeatedly. She didn't care why he had married her at that moment, she didn't even care that he didn't love her, it was enough that she was this close to him.

'Can we change the subject?' she asked pleadingly.

His mouth tightened, a muscle jerking in his jaw. 'No games, Marie-Claire,' he warned in a low voice. 'I've had enough of those to last me a lifetime.'

'I don't want to play games!' she replied, suddenly very tired, as a weak exhaustion crept up on her, hitting her so hard that she closed her eyes, leaning back against the wall. 'Where is your daughter?' she asked in a small voice, unable to cope any more with the dangerous tension of talking about themselves.

'She was asleep before we got home,' Lee replied. 'I put her straight to bed, a wise move, in the circumstances.'

'I'm so tired,' she whispered, hardly able to open her eyes. The light seemed harsher, too bright to cope with. She wasn't going to fight any more.

'You're exhausted,' he said gently, and lifting her into his arms, carried her to the bed. As he laid her down and began deftly sliding away her clothes, she fought him, imagining in her exhaustion that he was going to hurt her, her eyes enormous with drugged emotion.

Lee held down her arms, his face a blank mask. 'Damn you, Marie-Claire,' he muttered wearily, as though her fighting hurt him, 'I'm not going to hurt you—I'm not going to touch you.'

As he pulled the cool silken sheets over her almost

naked body, she whispered his name, half asleep now, hardly aware of what she was doing. He bent his dark head and touched his mouth to her forehead in reassurance. The firm gentle touch of his lips was the last thing she remembered as she drifted into a deep, thankfully dreamless sleep.

She didn't wake until very late the next morning, fighting to open her eyes, and a heavy lethargy settled over her as the events of the day before rolled through her wakening mind. She turned over slowly to find the bed empty, though the pillow next to hers bore the indentation of Lee's head. She moved so that she was lying where he had lain, and stared up at the ceiling, her eyes filling with hot, damnable tears.

The room was dark, the blinds still closed. Outside she could hear birdsong, the barking of a dog in the distance. Oh, Lee, she thought achingly, knowing that he must have slept next to her all night, that she had not known, that he had not touched her.

It was all such a mess! Tiredly she crawled out of bed and took a cool shower, allowing the pelting water to wash away the last traces of drugged sleep, then she dressed in jeans and a red jumper, brushing her hair until it shone, her actions numbly mechanical. She was not looking forward to facing her husband.

The house was quiet as she crept downstairs, but she heard high childish laughter coming from the kitchen, so she tentatively pushed open the door.

Lee sat indolently at the huge polished table, an open newspaper in front of him, laughing with a small slender little girl who had raven black hair and wide clear grey eyes. Laurie.

Marie-Claire watched Lee as she stood in the doorway unnoticed. Her heart lurched painfully at the love she saw in his eyes, at the warm smile that curved the firm line of his mouth.

Then, as though sensing her presence, he suddenly turned his head and saw her lurking apprehensively near the door. Their eyes met, and his hardened, blanking into expressionless steel as they slid the length of her body in slow appraisal.

'Come in,' he said smoothly, and she obeyed on legs that were trembling.

'It's so late—I didn't realise——' she said nervously.

Lee shrugged. 'You were exhausted, I thought it better to let you sleep.'

The little girl looked up at her as she came in. 'Who are you?' she demanded, jumping off her seat and running over to Marie-Claire, staring up at her with guileless curiosity.

She was an incredibly beautiful child, Marie-Claire thought, staring down at her. She had Lee's dark hair and grey eyes, but a delicate, perfect bone structure that Marie-Claire assumed was inherited from her mother.

'I'm Marie-Claire,' she introduced herself.

The little girl nodded. 'Daddy told me about you,' she said proudly.

'And you must be Laurie.'

'How do you know?' Laurie's eyes were wide.

'Your daddy told me about you, too,' Marie-Claire replied, her heart already lost to the warm beauty of the child.

'Are you Daddy's friend?'

The innocent question took Marie-Claire's breath away. She looked at Lee, shrinking from the cynical mockery in his grey eyes, unsure how to answer.

'Yes,' Lee answered for her, 'Marie-Claire is my friend.'

Laurie looked from her father to Marie-Claire, then back, saying confidentially to him, 'She's pretty, isn't she? I like her.'

Lee's eyes met Marie-Claire's again. 'She's very pretty,' he agreed in a low husky voice.

Marie-Claire shivered at his tone, thinking she must have imagined it as he continued briskly, 'Coffee?'

She nodded, watching him rise indolently to his feet to pour some for her. 'Are you hungry?' he asked, setting the cup of fresh coffee in front of her.

'I had an egg,' Laurie cut in, seating herself next to Marie-Claire. 'Are you going to have an egg?'

Marie-Claire smiled and looked at Lee. 'I won't have anything, thanks, I'm not very hungry.' She couldn't have touched a thing, the very thought of food made her feel sick.

'As you wish.' He turned away, pouring a glass of milk for Laurie, and she watched his every movement, a terrible aching need churning in her stomach.

This morning he was dressed formally in an expensively-cut dark blue suit and a thin pale shirt. The jacket was hung on his chair, his waistcoat unbuttoned, emphasising the powerful male virility of his body.

That he adored his beautiful little daughter was obvious, and as Marie-Claire watched them together, her heart ached with a wistful longing. The bond of love and respect between them shone brightly in the wintry kitchen, and Marie-Claire found herself hoping against hope that the courts would allow them to stay together.

Laurie was supremely happy with her father, that was beyond doubt, a happiness that lit her delicate little face whenever she looked at him. Laurie drank her milk, obediently sitting at the table, still eyeing Marie-Claire.

'Are you going to live with us?' she asked suddenly, licking her lips.

Marie-Claire nodded, aware that Lee's eyes were

fixed upon her, aware of the sudden stillness tensing his powerful body. 'Yes, I'm going to live with you,' she answered shakily, knowing at that precise second that she couldn't leave, not until she knew that Laurie was going to stay with Lee.

She loved the child already, she was so much like her father. She did not look at Lee, afraid of what he might read in her eyes.

'You won't go away like Naomi did?' the child persisted worriedly.

Marie-Claire frowned, surprised that Laurie called her mother by her christian name. 'No, I'll stay for as long as you like,' she said, smiling as she watched the child visibly relaxing.

'Oh, goody!' Laurie happily finished her milk.

Glancing covertly at Lee, Marie-Claire found him staring at his daughter's shining bent head with a bleakness in his eyes that trapped the breath in her throat. She found herself wondering about his ex-wife and the circumstances of their divorce. It had obviously been bitter, otherwise Naomi wouldn't be contesting the custody ruling. It was difficult to imagine anybody wanting to separate Lee from his daughter.

She watched him as he walked over to the child, and lifted her into his strong arms. She listened as he explained to Laurie that he and Marie-Claire were now married. He did it calmly and tenderly, using words the little girl could understand, and although she cursed herself, Marie-Claire found her eyes filling with tears, the scene before her so poignant, so beautiful.

'Is Marie-Claire my new mummy, then?' Laurie demanded hopefully, when he had finished explaining the situation.

'She might be, one day,' Lee replied carefully.

'Will you be my new mummy?' the child persisted, the question now directed at Marie-Claire, her grey eyes almost desperate. Lee was silent, his glance narrowing. It was up to her to answer and she didn't know how to.

'Let's just be friends for now, shall we?' she said very gently.

Laurie stared at her, wide-eyed, considering the proposition. 'Okay,' she finally conceded with a smile.

Marie-Claire relaxed her taut body on a sigh of relief. Children asked such impossible questions, and what else could she have said? She couldn't make promises to Laurie that she might not be able to keep. The child was far too intelligent to be fobbed off with prevarication.

At that moment Mrs Ingram, Lee's housekeeper, arrived, dispelling the tension in the kitchen as she apologised profusely for her lateness, explaining that her niece, who was staying with her, had scalded her hand just as she was leaving to go to work.

'That's all right, Mrs Ingram,' Lee smiled soothingly at the older woman, who was eyeing Marie-Claire with open curiosity. 'Let me introduce you to my wife, Marie-Claire.'

Introductions were duly made, and the two women shook hands. Mrs Ingram was in her late fifties, small and round with kindly eyes, and Laurie obviously adored her.

'I'm so happy for you both,' she said mistily as she released Marie-Claire's hand.

Laurie danced round them all, graceful and excited. 'Marie-Claire's my new mummy!' she told Mrs Ingram delightedly.

'Laurie!' Lee's voice was stern.

The child smiled up at him angelically. 'Well, we're friends for now, but she'll be my new mummy soon,' she amended brightly, catching hold of the house-keeper's hand.

Lee slid his arm around Marie-Claire's shoulders and she stiffened in surprise. 'I want to talk to you,' he murmured, and bending his head, brushed her temple with his lips.

It was a show, she realised painfully, her stupid heart leaping at his casual touch. It was all for Mrs Ingram's benefit, and it was working; the housekeeper smiled broadly as she watched them.

In the warm book-lined study, Lee shrugged into the jacket of his suit, his unreadable eyes flicking over her.

'Thanks for treating Laurie so kindly,' he said quietly.

'That's okay—she's so lovely,' Marie-Claire replied awkwardly, flushing deeply at his gratitude.

'I'm sorry if all that business about her mother embarrassed you.'

'I wasn't sure what to say,' Marie-Claire said falteringly.

'I know. I think you ought to know about her mother,' Lee said expressionlessly. 'It will help you to understand, and cope with all the questions.'

'Oh—no, really——' She wasn't sure she wanted to know, it was bound to be painful.

'Yes, Marie-Claire.' He smiled slightly. 'Sit down.'

She perched nervously on one of the plush leather armchairs, while Lee sat on the edge of the huge mahogany desk.

'Naomi is a dancer, she never wanted children,' he began flatly, without preamble. 'Laurie's conception was a mistake, as far as Naomi was concerned and she resented it. She hated being pregnant and she hated having to give up her career, however temporarily, to have the baby. She blamed me, but worse—she blamed Laurie. She seemed determined to treat the child as though she was somebody else's—insisting that Laurie called her by her christian name—almost denying the child's existence.' He paused, his eyes blank with anger, raking a hand through the darkness of his hair.

'Right from the start, she would palm Laurie off with anybody who would have her, while she visited her lovers, her friends. Oh, I'm not saying I was blameless, I was abroad a great deal of the time and I guess in that way I neglected her just as badly. But you see, Laurie has never really had a mother who cared, and now she's old enough to understand that all her friends at school have loving mothers, and that she, through no fault of her own, is somehow different from everybody else, she's desperate to change the situation. Hence the embarrassing questions.'

Marie-Claire listened in silence, her tender heart crying for the lonely little girl. How could Naomi have been so cruel? she wondered painfully. She looked at Lee. His hard face gave nothing at all away, but he must have been hurt by his wife's infidelity, by the fact that she obviously didn't care for his child. He must have been, even though he looked as though none of it had ever touched him.

'I'm sorry,' she whispered, knowing how inadequate it was. 'I'm so sorry. I just don't understand——' She broke off, realising that it was not her place to comment on what was, after all, really none of her business.

'How a woman can completely disregard the existence and the feelings of her own child?' Lee finished for her, his voice bitter, very grim.

'No, I. . . .' Colour scorched Marie-Claire's cheeks as she tried to protest, but Lee shook his dark head, silencing her.

'God only knows the answer to that. Naomi, like a lot of other women of her kind, is driven by greed. She wants money and freedom and excitement, and playing the role of doting mother really doesn't fit in with her image of herself.'

He stood up in one lithe angry movement, glancing at the watch on his tanned wrist. 'I have to drive into the city, I have some business to attend to.'

Marie-Claire stood up too, and walked towards the door, thinking herself dismissed. But Lee blocked her way, staring down into her sad eyes.

He smiled, and bending his head, brushed her surprised mouth with his own, parting her lips in a fierce hard kiss.

'I'll see you later.'

He had gone before she could say a word, and she stood staring after him, her fingers pressed to her lips.

She knew she wouldn't leave, she couldn't leave now. She had made her promises to Laurie, and Lee knew she wouldn't break them.

CHAPTER SEVEN

A WEEK passed. A good week, Marie-Claire supposed warily as she walked with Laurie by the icy river that ran through the village, one dark afternoon.

Friendship was growing all the time between Laurie and herself; the child was almost clinging to her, grabbing eagerly at the friendship as though starving. And Marie-Claire, although she tried desperately hard not to, found herself giving the child all the love she could not give to Lee.

She thought of her husband now, and that familiar painful ache squeezed her heart. He was away on business in New York and was not due back for a few days.

They had parted in angry silence after a furious row the night before he left. The desperate tension crackling between them that evening had somehow exploded into fury at Marie-Claire's casual unthinking mention of Chris's name.

Suddenly they had been facing each other as bitter enemies, Lee as cold and as hard as ice, cutting her to ribbons with his cynical cruelty, while she had shouted her frustrations at him, her tearful accusations. And in the end, driven beyond anger, Lee had reached for her, his strong hands rough, his mouth violently savage as it possessed hers.

It had been his intention to punish, she had known that, but his intensity was a powerful aphrodisiac, and her response had been as overwhelming and as violent as his. She had revelled in his strength, his mastery. As they lay entwined on the soft rug in front of the blazing fire, Lee's mouth had lost its violence in hunger against the soft shoulders bared by his lean seeking fingers.

She had moaned as he touched her breasts, whispering his name, lost to the desire that had been spiralling out of control inside her body, her only reality, Lee's warm smooth skin beneath her hands, the cool urgent touch of his mouth.

'Ah, Marie-Claire,' he had murmured unevenly against her throat, 'you only have to touch me and I burn up for you.'

The words had sunk slowly into her consciousness, bringing back that other reality, the cold harsh world where Lee didn't love her, had only married her because he needed a wife, and perhaps because he desired her body. And with that return to painful sanity, she had stiffened in his arms, the desire shrivelling quickly into a hard pain that had left her passive, unresponsive and crying silently against his body.

She had known he was angry, when he felt her tears, the deathly stillness of her body beneath his, and she had known that he was misinterpreting, misunderstanding her lightning change from yielding desire to cold rejection.

He had left her with a brutal cruelty, with words that had cut straight to her heart, and she had not slept that night, tossing fretfully in the huge bed, wondering where he was.

The following morning they had met by accident on the stairs.

She had flinched from that meeting, because she had been expecting to avoid it, but had been unable to stop herself staring at him with hungry eyes. He had looked tired, strained, his eyes holding a desolate bleakness that had hurt her.

They had stared at each other in tense silence, and Marie-Claire had known bitter regret at what she had said in anger, the night before. She had also admitted the wish that they had made love, had spent the night in each other's arms. That desire should not have been denied, and had it not been, perhaps it would have made things better, easier, because God knew, it was like a disease ravaging both of them.

She had wanted to say something. She had wanted to explain, to apologise.

'Lee. . . .' she had started bravely, but the words hadn't come. He had stared at her in brooding silence for a moment, then had said,

'I'm sorry about last night—I should never have touched you. I guess I——' He had shrugged, raking a tense weary hand through his hair.

'Don't,' she had begged, suddenly close to tears. 'Please, don't. . . .'

Moments later he had gone, and it had been Mrs Ingram who had later informed her that he had gone to New York on urgent business. He had not even told her that.

'Look! Marie-Claire—look——!' Laurie's excited voice diverted her miserable train of thought, bringing her back to the present. The little girl was pointing at three bedraggled ducks crouching on the frost-covered river bank.

Marie-Claire looked, forcing herself to smile and explain to Laurie that their feathers kept them warm, and that they weren't sad or cold, but that ducks were used to winter weather.

They walked on, hand in hand, and Marie-Claire stared blindly up at the dark misty trees, at the silver-grey sky. She loved the winter, the cold air, the hard frosty ground, the dark afternoons, and today the harshness suited her mood.

She was longing to see Lee again, every morning praying for his return; when he was away like this, she ached for him. It didn't matter that he did not love her; if he still wanted her, that would be enough.

You only get one short life, she thought fiercely, and right now, I'm prepared to take anything he'll give me. Her love was strong enough for both of them. Surely it was strong enough to break down the barriers that had grown so quickly between them.

Her mind was whirling away as Laurie chattered on and on, and she answered the little girl brightly, even though her thoughts were elsewhere.

Lee had telephoned once. She had been out shopping. Mrs Ingram had spoken to him. From what Marie-Claire had gathered, he had only wanted to know about his daughter. The housekeeper had not been surprised or suspicious, she assumed that Lee rang Marie-Claire at night. She imagined that they were the perfect couple, and had said as much to Marie-Claire, which meant that Lee's plan had worked. To the outside world, they *were* the perfect couple, and even Mrs Ingram didn't know that Marie-Claire spent every night crying alone in her huge empty bed, sick with longing for a husband who did not care.

Oh, but Lee was clever! He had trapped her so securely, iron chains couldn't have kept her better. He must have known how she and Laurie would have reacted to each other. He must have known that she wouldn't be able to leave once she had seen his daughter. And she couldn't even blame him for it. 'I'll do anything and everything in my power to keep Laurie with me,' he had said, and as soon as she had seen Laurie, she had known why. They belonged together.

She sighed, pushing back her silky hair. It was an

impossible situation, one in which she was inextricably trapped by her undeniable love for Lee and her growing feelings for his child.

She could think about it for twenty-four hours a day and it wouldn't get her anywhere. Her thoughts ran in circles and there was no answer. All she knew for certain was that she would stay for as long as Lee needed her. There was no pride in her love for him, it was a love too deep, too strong and all-encompassing for that particular luxury.

She was still deep in thought as they reached the edge of the woods that bordered the village, and she hardly noticed the huge red setter bounding out of the trees towards them.

But Laurie noticed, and with a cry of delight pulled her tiny gloved hand out of Marie-Claire's, and rushed over to the dog.

'It's Günther!' she exclaimed excitedly.

About to speak, Marie-Claire was silenced by the appearance of a tall man, obviously the dog's owner, walking towards them.

'Hello, Laurie.' He smiled at the child. 'I didn't know you were back.'

He was ruggedly attractive, in his late forties, Marie-Claire would have estimated, his dark hair greying at the temples, his blue eyes kind and world-weary.

'Let me introduce myself,' he said to Marie-Claire, his glance appreciative as it rested on her slender form. 'Harrison Sinclair.' He held out his hand.

'I'm Marie-Claire Harper,' she smiled as they shook hands.

'Marie-Claire is married to my daddy,' Laurie cut in proudly, still stroking the dog's silky fur.

'Really? I heard Lee was married. How are you settling in?'

He was open and friendly and Marie-Claire liked him immediately. 'Fine,' she replied, faint colour staining her cheeks. 'It's lovely here.'

She looked at her watch, her natural shyness preventing her from saying too much to him, because he was a stranger. Laurie was making up for it, though, chattering away nineteen to the dozen, while the red dog wagged its tail at her side.

'We'd better be getting back,' Mairie-Claire suggested to Laurie at last. 'It will be dark soon.'

'Okay,' the little girl smiled obediently.

'I'm going your way, mind if I walk with you?' Harrison Sinclair asked charmingly.

'Of course not, Mr Sinclair, we'd be glad of your company,' she replied, her dark eyes smiling.

'Harrison, please. I can't bear formality.'

Laurie insisted on taking both adults' hands as they walked back, and Günther shot ahead, boundless with energy.

Something was nagging away in Marie-Claire's mind as they chatted, and she suddenly realised what it was. 'Sinclair,' she said thoughtfully. 'Are you by any chance related to Melissa Sinclair?'

Harrison's blue eyes met hers, wryly amused. 'Melissa is my wife,' he explained slowly.

'Oh, I had no idea——' After what Melissa had said about herself and Lee, Marie-Claire felt flustered, embarrassed by the revelation.

'You've met her, I take it?' It was almost as though he knew what she was thinking.

Marie-Claire flushed. 'Yes, she dropped in to see L—us, the day we got back from Switzerland.' She had nearly said Lee, and could have bitten off her tongue. Harrison was such a good man, it was hard to believe that he had a wife like Melissa, and she wanted to cover up the near-slip, launching into fast speech.

'It's quite a coincidence, isn't it? Although I suppose in a village this size——'

'It's all right,' Harrison cut in quietly. 'Fortunately, in common with the rest of the village, I'm very well aware of Melissa's indiscretions.' He was smiling, trying to ease her embarrassment, but it only made her feel worse.

So it was true, even Harrison knew about Melissa and Lee! Colour scorched her cheeks, and she lowered her head, not knowing what to say, fighting the terrible pain inside her.

'Hey, come on, don't feel bad.' Harrison tilted up her chin, his blue eyes holding hers. 'How about a pact? We'll agree not to talk about Melissa, right? Round here, it's a subject I'm used to avoiding.' His voice was light, conciliatory, and she nodded in agreement, feeling strangely sorry for him, and curious too. He knew of his wife's infidelities and seemed able to accept them as merely an embarrassment, a topic of conversation to be avoided. Half of her could understand it, wasn't she doing the same with Lee?

Luckily Laurie diverted his attention at that moment and they were back at the house in no time at all.

'Come in for tea, Uncle Harrison,' Laurie demanded beguilingly, as they reached the garden gate.

'Well——' Harrison hesitated, looking at Marie-Claire, and she was forced to say: 'Yes, please do, you'd be very welcome.'

'Then thank you, I will.'

He seemed pleased by the invitation, and Marie-Claire hated herself for her lack of enthusiasm. He was a nice man, and it was hardly his fault if his wife was having an affair with her husband.

In the kitchen, Mrs Ingram greeted him as an old

friend, and Marie-Claire knew she had done the right thing. They all sat round the table, eating freshly-baked scones with jam, and drinking tea. Outside the winter evening closed in, and the wind began to howl in the bare trees. Marie-Claire looked around the warm kitchen, at the open fire, the wooden dressers and shining pans, the quarry-tiled floor, and felt strangely content, at home.

'I'm going to ask Daddy if I can have a dog like Günther,' Laurie announced, stuffing her scone into her mouth as though she were starving. 'When will he be back?'

Aware that Harrison was watching her, Marie-Claire let the dark curtain of her hair swing forward over her face, as she said almost evenly, 'I don't know—soon, I expect.'

'When's soon?' Laurie persisted innocently, watching Günther licking up the crumbs she held out to him.

'I know a farm where they've got a litter of puppies, just like Günther,' Harrison intervened smoothly, staring at Marie-Claire. 'We'll go and see them some time, shall we?'

'Oh, yes—yes, please!' Laurie was enchanted by the suggestion, and was still talking about it when Mrs Ingram whisked her away upstairs for her bath, the housekeeper leaving Marie-Claire instructions to make another pot of tea for Harrison.

She did as she was told, happy to fiddle with the kettle and the teapot, afraid of what she had given away under Laurie's persistent questioning.

'What do you do for a living, Harrison?' she asked lightly, as she spooned the fragrant tea into the warmed pot.

'I'm a writer—biographies,' he replied briefly.

'That must be fascinating,' she enthused as she sat down again.

'You look tired,' he said, changing the subject, a quiet concern in his voice.

Marie-Claire poured the tea. Somehow his kind undemanding sympathy undermined the fragile expensive barrier of calmness she was presenting to the world. Yes, she was tired, desperately tired. She hadn't had a peaceful night's sleep for ages and she was well aware of the damning dark shadows beneath her eyes.

'I suppose it's all this fresh air—I'm used to living in the dirty city,' she replied with a brittle little smile.

Harrison was silent, his expression telling her that he didn't believe a word. He was trying to help, offering friendship. She felt the need to make some further explanation, still fighting to keep up her barriers. 'I suppose I. . . .' She felt her voice breaking and to her utter horror, burst into tears, some gentleness in Harrison's eyes releasing the tension and emotion she had been damming up during the past week. It was totally embarrassing to cry like this in front of a virtual stranger, but she couldn't stop for the life of her.

Harrison didn't seem in the least perturbed, however. He calmly handed her a clean handkerchief from his jacket pocket.

'I'm sorry. . . .' she sniffed, dabbing angrily at her wet face.

'Don't be. Cry all you want to—it's good for you,' Harrison said kindly. 'And when you've dried your eyes you can tell me why, if you like. You'll find that I'm a very sympathetic listener.'

Marie-Claire smiled, a thin watery smile that he pounced on. 'There you are—much better!'

'You're so kind,' she said weakly.

'I'm always kind to beautiful young women,' Harrison assured her, his blue eyes humorous. 'And you're particularly beautiful. Lee's a very lucky man.'

It was intended as a compliment, but somehow it made her wince with pain.

The astute Harrison, watching her carefully, saw that pain and said, 'I take it that Lee is at the bottom of all this, and judging by your reactions when you found out that Melissa is my wife, I suspect that she has something to do with it as well.'

Marie-Claire's eyes widened at his perception, giving her away, but she said nothing. How could she tell him? What could she say?

'Tell me,' he prompted quietly, 'I may be able to help.'

'I can't,' she replied unhappily. 'I really can't.'

Harrison lit a cigarette, offering her one which she took thankfully. Then he fixed her with shrewd eyes.

'Sweet, loyal Marie-Claire—I'll take a guess, then, shall I?'

She stared at him worriedly, saying nothing, and he continued, 'You said Melissa had been round here, yes?' Marie-Claire nodded, still silent. 'And she told you, or hinted, that she was having an affair with your husband?' he hazarded quite calmly, quite unworriedly, and Marie-Claire was shocked, so shocked that she heard herself saying,

'How did you know?' before she checked the words, her hand clamping over her mouth in horror.

Harrison smiled. 'It wasn't difficult—I half guessed the moment you asked about her.' He drew deeply on his cigarette. 'We've been married for five years and we understand each other very well indeed. Sure, Melissa has affairs with other men—she needs the reassurance that she's still a beautiful woman— reassurance that I can't give her because we're married, because the familiarity of our relationship somehow precludes the truth. It isn't enough any more that I tell her how beautiful she is, but I love her, you see, and she always comes back to me—she never really cares for the man she sleeps with. Oh, it isn't a perfect situation by any means, and I know I fool myself a lot of the time, but I'm prepared to accept it, if it's the price I have to pay for her.'

Marie-Claire listened, achingly sorry for him, even though he seemed perfectly happy.

The idea of sharing Lee with other women was intolerable to her. That was why Melissa's clever insinuations had hurt her so much.

'I don't know what to say,' she admitted at last in a husky voice.

'Don't say anything, just listen,' Harrison said with a smile. 'I'm prepared to swear that Melissa isn't having an affair with Lee. Oh, I know she wouldn't turn down the chance—she's told me that herself—but I know Lee, and he wouldn't offer her that chance. He's not interested, he never has been, and that's what jars on Melissa's vanity, her insecurity. You really mustn't worry, Marie-Claire. Melissa has never got near Lee, she never will; he doesn't want her. Your husband is strong, a man of integrity. He's my friend, and that fact alone would keep him away from Melissa.' He spoke with such certainty that she believed him, and it was like a weight falling from her shoulders. She looked at him, her eyes jewel-bright.

'It's true,' he repeated, with a calm smile. 'Believe it.'

'I do, and right at this moment I feel like kissing you!'

Behind her, the kitchen door swung silently open, as she spoke, and Lee's sardonic voice remarked, 'I trust you won't be taking my wife up on that breathless offer, Harrison.'

Marie-Claire's head jerked round. She hadn't been expecting him today and her heart lifted with pleasure.

'I wouldn't dare,' Harrison said laughingly as he got to his feet. 'I have to be going anyway.'

Marie-Claire said goodbye, knowing that she had found a special friend, and Lee showed him out.

She waited in the kitchen, sitting very still, her heart pounding as he came back.

'Is there any coffee?' he asked, tiredly, flexing his shoulder muscles as he sat down.

He looked exhausted, she thought, staring at him. He looked leaner, the bones of his face harder, more gaunt, and his grey eyes held a smouldering intensity when he looked at her.

'I'll make some.' She jumped up quickly and switched on the percolator. 'Can ... can I get you something to eat?' she asked falteringly.

'Mrs Ingram is very well paid for doing the cooking,' Lee replied laconically, pulling off his tie, shrugging off the jacket of his suit and flinging it over the back of his chair.

'I like cooking,' Marie-Claire protested, hurt, unable to drag her eyes away from those tense powerful shoulders.

'It's okay, I'm not hungry,' he said, a slight smile curving the edges of his mouth.

He was watching her, she realised, as she reached into the cupboard for clean cups, and his cool grey eyes were fixed with intensity on every movement she made.

She poured the coffee, strong and black, how he liked it, and her hands trembled. The silence in the kitchen was so heavy it was almost tangible, the invisible walls between them reaching as high as the sky.

Marie-Claire nervously licked her lips. 'You look tired,' she said gently.

Lee raked a hand through his thick dark hair. 'I am.

Dammit, I seem to have been travelling non-stop for the past forty-eight hours!'

'Oh.' She didn't know what to say to him. They were like strangers, she thought miserably, strangers who could never communicate. It was all so wrong, especially when her heart was singing with happiness because he was back.

Lee swallowed back his coffee. 'And you?' he queried expressionlessly. 'How are you, Marie-Claire?'

'I'm very well,' she answered, too quickly, too nervously.

'Little liar, you've been crying,' he contradicted coolly. 'What the hell did Harrison say to make you cry?'

She looked away from him, biting her lip. 'He didn't make me cry,' she said stiffly. 'I made myself cry.' She paused. 'Have you seen Laurie?'

Lee's eyes narrowed. 'I'll see Laurie later,' he said, dismissing her diversionary tactics. 'She's already asleep—I saw Mrs Ingram on my way in. Right now, I'm more concerned with you.'

'You have no need to be. As I said, I'm fine.'

Lee stood up, indolently stretching his arms above his head, before pouring himself more coffee. 'For God's sake, Marie-Claire,' he said very softly, 'stop playing games! I'm too tired to fence with you.' He looked at her, slowly appraising every inch of her, from head to toe, then he said, 'Apart from the fact that you've been crying, I'd say you haven't been eating properly, and you certainly haven't been sleeping well.'

'Very clever!' she retorted, turning away from those probing grey eyes. He saw too much, and she didn't want him to see anything.

She stood by the dark window, staring blindly into

the winter night, her body strangely weak. 'I don't know why you're asking me all these questions, if you already know the answers.'

She was angry—angry with herself for her breathless response to him, and angry with him because he didn't care enough.

'Is it such hell, living here?' His low husky voice was right behind her, making her jump. She hadn't noticed him moving. He always moved so silently, like a dark dangerous panther.

'Sometimes,' she whispered honestly. She felt Lee's hand touching her hair and shivered, afraid that she would give her need for him away, gasping as he tangled his long fingers in it, pulling round her head so that she faced him. She stared frantically into eyes as hard as steel.

'Don't worry,' he drawled coldly. 'You make your abhorrence of my touch quite apparent, and I've never understood the appeal of rape.'

Marie-Claire felt the aching blockage of tears in her throat. If only he knew! It was unbelievable how quickly their relationship had deteriorated, how anger could burn up like flame, so savagely, so destructively.

'Are you still aching to leave, Marie-Claire?' he asked smoothly, staring down into her wide, fear-tinged eyes with a blank detached curiosity. 'Are you still longing for your ex-fiancé?'

She stood perfectly still. The fingers twisted in the thick silk of her hair were quite gentle, yet she knew if she moved they would hurt her. In the silence she could hear the steady ticking of the old wooden clock on the mantelpiece, the roaring of the fire in the iron grate, the pounding of her own heart in her ears. The kitchen was warm and bright, no place for the remorseless bitterness that clawed between them. 'I haven't seen Chris,' she said shakily, wondering why she had ever let Lee believe that she still cared. She didn't have that much pride now, but it had gone too far for her to back out of.

'No? A missed opportunity, my love,' Lee drawled, his narrowed eyes effortlessly holding hers. 'And an opportunity that I don't intend to give you again.'

'I don't understand. . . .'

A bitter smile touched his lips. 'Think about it,' he advised.

She did, and the realisation shocked her. 'You expected me to leave while you were away.'

'It wouldn't have surprised me,' came the cool bitter reply.

'But I promised Laurie that I'd stay——' she protested weakly.

'And is that why you're still here? Because of Laurie?' He was very still, his powerful body strangely tense as he waited for her answer. It had all been a test, she thought wildly. A cold deliberate test.

'Yes,' she replied flatly, unable to reveal her true feelings. 'Yes, yes, *yes*!'

His fingers tightened painfully in her hair, and she heard him swearing softly under his breath. She stared at his mouth, the firm masculine line of it, and her stomach turned over. If she had not known better, she might have imagined that she had hurt him; in truth, she knew that she had only pushed him beyond anger.

'Well, at least you're honest,' he said at last, in a coldly amused voice, and she knew that he had regained control of himself.

'And that's all you want, isn't it?' she flung back, stung by that calm amusement. It was all so easy for him!

His dark eyes mocked her. 'You'd be surprised,' he said softly, his meaning clear.

'I doubt it!' she retorted, but her courage was failing

at the sudden heat in his eyes. She wanted to hit out, to break the nerve-racking tension one way or the other.

'I must have been mad to marry you—it was too soon——' she broke off, tears glazing her eyes with brilliance, as she watched the ominous tightening of his mouth. 'Don't misunderstand,' she begged desperately. 'You know what I mean.'

Lee closed his eyes for a second, a grim weariness etching the hard lines of his face.

'Unfortunately, Marie-Claire, I know exactly what you mean, but I can't let you go—you'd better remember that and accept it.'

She remembered it very well, she thought hysterically. He needed her for the custody case. He needed her so much, he was willing to make both their lives unbearable. How could she go on living with him, when she loved him so much, when she ached so desperately for his touch night and day?

'You must hate me,' she said brokenly, the tears running uncontrollably down her face.

Lee's dark brows rose, and his smile was gentle, catching the breath in her throat. 'Hate? I could never hate you, my love,' he said, his voice softening. 'God knows, you've been on my mind every minute since I left for New York.'

'Because you thought I'd run away?' she sniffed belligerently.

'What did Harrison tell you?' he countered, frowning slightly, his hands sliding to her shoulders.

She shivered under his touch, aware of his nearness, his hard male strength. She was tired of lying. All she wanted was to fling herself into his arms and beg him to make love to her.

'He told me that you and Melissa are not having an affair,' she revealed in a shaky whisper.

'I could have told you that,' said Lee, smiling at her with a charm that confused her even as it warmed her frozen heart.

'I was afraid to ask you,' she admitted, her heart pounding as he bent his head, erotically licking away her cold tears with his tongue.

'Melissa has made her invitation crystal clear, but I'm really not at all interested—as I've already told her. She's a cold spiteful bitch and she's made Harrison's life hell,' he murmured.

'He must love her so much, though,' Marie-Claire said, trembling.

'She's got him on his knees,' Lee replied cynically. 'And she'll keep him there for the rest of his life.'

'Poor Harrison, it's so unfair.' Marie-Claire's eyes were very sad.

Lee's mouth twisted mockingly. 'Feel sorry for yourself, Marie-Claire, because I don't intend to sleep alone tonight.'

She backed away, wide-eyed, her body trembling at the hungry desire suddenly smouldering in the depths of his eyes, a weak responsive heat aching in the pit of her stomach. 'No——' she began fretfully, denying herself more than him.

'I want you,' Lee said unevenly, his breathing quick and sharp in the quiet of the room. 'I want you so badly that it's tearing me apart. You're my wife, Marie-Claire, and I need you in my bed tonight— every damn night!'

The husky words turned her legs to jelly. 'You tricked me,' she muttered breathlessly, still backing away.

'Oh, no, if you've been harbouring any illusions, they're of your own imagination,' he replied, his darkening eyes burning into hers. 'I've never pretended that I didn't want you.'

His glance rested on her heaving breasts as she fought to control the inflammable need that was threatening to overwhelm all her caution, all her self-preserving common sense. 'Lee, don't—I can't—not without love,' she whispered, watching him, hypnotised, knowing that she had made him angry again by her denial.

He walked towards her, a tall dark powerful man with grey eyes that stripped away her every defence, eyes that glittered with deep desire.

He trapped her so easily, reaching for her in hard silence, his mouth touching hers, parting her lips with a kiss that reinforced the message in his eyes.

Marie-Claire moaned softly, unable to control her violent response. She had been waiting for this moment, waiting so long, she had felt she was going mad. She kissed him back, her lips moving under his, and she felt him shudder as she slid her hands across his wide tense shoulders, fingers caressing.

She felt the heavy strength of his arms holding her like bands of steel, her own body yielding softly against the hardness of his.

The kiss went on for ever, deepening and deepening until she was drowning in pleasure and need. Lee's cool erotic mouth touched her eyelids, her temples, her earlobes, touched her gently with a passion as hot as the sun, making love to her with a possessive need that made her tremble feverishly, unable to deny him anything.

'I missed you,' she admitted, on a soft sigh.

'And I you,' he muttered possessively against her skin. 'You wouldn't believe how much!' And when his mouth parted hers again, they clung together desperately, straining closer, closer, her aching breasts crushed to the unyielding hardness of his chest.

His long fingers stroked over her body, tracing the soft curves with a hard urgency reinforced by the tension of his muscles.

It wasn't enough, she thought drowsily, achingly, her fingers fumbling with the buttons of his waistcoat. She wanted to touch his smooth tanned flesh, she wanted to rub her palms against the rough hair that matted his chest. She wanted to kiss his powerful body, taste the firm beauty of his skin. God, how she needed him!

Then suddenly everything changed, the whole world seemed to shift. The waistcoat open, she slid her hands inside, reaching for his silken shirt. They were caught, trapped by Lee's own hands.

He pulled them roughly away from his chest, leaving her dazed, shocked as she saw the desire fading from his grey eyes. His lean fingers framed her face, tense against her skin. She felt her colour rising as he forced her to meet the cynical contempt in his eyes.

'You're right,' he said harshly, 'Without love it doesn't mean a damn thing.' It was as though he had never held her, never kissed her or touched her, and her body stiffened with icy pain, as he added, 'And I won't let you use me as a substitute for your ex-fiancé, Marie-Claire, desirable as you are!'

She closed her eyes as he released her, and when she opened them again, he was gone.

It was like a dream, a fantasy that had never existed.

The clock was still ticking steadily, the fire still roaring, but the thunder in her ears was not a heart beating with excitement and desire, it was a heart beating with pained, confused humiliation.

CHAPTER EIGHT

Two days later, the telephone rang as Marie-Claire was drinking her breakfast coffee. It was Ran, his voice faint and faraway as he greeted her.

'How's married life, dear cousin?' he demanded jovially.

Lost in the pleasure of hearing from him, Marie-Claire answered automatically. 'I love it—you ought to try it!'

The chance to confide had been thrown away, and Ran was the only person she could have confided in, she realised, as they chatted. Why was she lying? Why was she pretending? In truth, things were worse than ever. She forced herself to listen to what Ran was saying.

'Don't worry, I'm taking that advice, I *am* going to try it. That's why I'm ringing, I wanted you to be the first to know. Bettina and I are engaged,' he revealed happily. 'I asked her last night and, incredibly, she accepted.'

It wasn't exactly a big surprise, but it melted Marie-Claire's heart with happiness. 'Oh, Ran, I'm *so* pleased!' she congratulated him, glad that at last he had found a woman he loved, and who loved him in return. His exultant happiness seemed to rush infectiously along the telephone cables as they talked about the wedding.

The date was set for July and they were holding the ceremony in London so that Bettina's family could attend.

'Do you think Lee would be my best man?' Ran asked hopefully.

'I'm sure he would—he'd be honoured,' she replied, the very thought of her husband hurting deeply.

'Will you ask him? I'll be getting in touch of course, but you can work your charm on him first.'

What charm? she wondered cynically. Lee had made it crystal clear that he was immune to any charm she might possess!

'I don't think he'll need much persuading,' she said, as lightly as she could.

Ran's happiness somehow brought her own misery into sharp relief. She tried to hide it, but it was a twenty-four-hour-a-day job, pretending to the world that her marriage was perfect. She had to try so hard, she could almost believe it herself sometimes.

Before Ran rang off, she asked about Rima and James, and he told her that they were due to leave Switzerland the following day. 'So you'll probably see them within the week. Rima was asking about you yesterday,' he said, his voice fading as the line crackled loudly. It was something to look forward to, seeing Rima again. Marie-Claire missed her companionship.

As she replaced the receiver five minutes later, thoughts of her time spent in Switzerland crammed her mind. Everything had been so good there. She and Lee had been so happy, so close. Had that been a dream?

She remembered their trip to Gornergrat and her eyes filled with tears. Had she really thought she could take what she wanted from the world? Use it as it had used her? Had she really imagined she could control her affair with Lee, and emerge unscathed?

Switzerland had been magical, charmed and untouched by sadness. The world had fallen around her ears as soon as she returned to England. But she still loved Lee. The love that had blossomed so explosively, so sweetly in Switzerland was deepening daily, woven inextricably into her soul, so that she would love him with all her heart until the day she died, she was utterly sure of that.

And that was why she was so raw, so exposed to his cynical contempt, his cruelty.

In a desperate effort to protect herself, she had let him believe that she was still involved with Chris. That impulse had been a big mistake because she couldn't back out of it. Whatever she said now, Lee would still believe she was involved. She had been so foolish, so frightened of love, of life, of taking a chance. Fool, fool, *fool*!

She got up and poured herself another cup of coffee, and reaching for a cigarette, lit it and drew on it deeply. She walked over to the windows, curling herself up on the cushioned window seat. Outside, the sun was glistening hazily on the faint, cold layer of snow that had fallen overnight. The gardens and trees were bare, wintry, very beautiful. There was a swing hanging from one of the old trees, the green-painted seat white with frost. It looked stiff, empty, just waiting for a child to use it, to bring it back to life. Marie-Claire sighed. Sweet, beautiful Laurie had complicated things beyond belief. She couldn't leave now that the child was so attached to her—and vice versa. She couldn't believe that Lee hadn't known she would be lost as soon as she saw Laurie. If there was any way she could help Laurie to stay with Lee, she had to try.

It was difficult to understand why the unknown Naomi should want to split them up. From what Laurie had said about her mother from time to time, there didn't seem to be any particular affection between them.

She finished her coffee, moving restlessly. If only Lee loved her, if only he cared! If only he hadn't

married her for the wrong reasons. She closed her
eyes. How many times had she thought that? There
was no point. She couldn't survive on 'ifs'. He didn't
care, he probably never would, and she had to accept
that, however hard it was, however painful.

So what would she do? Spend the rest of her life
with a man who didn't love her, in the vain hope that
some day he might come to care?

At that moment, even that bleak proposition seemed
better than a life alone, never seeing him, because she
knew that there would never be anybody else, and
while she lived here at least she could hope, at least
she could know the painful joy of seeing him every
day, the bittersweet pleasure of his nearness.

God, she was a fool! She should have known. She
should have realised and not ignored those instincts
that had warned her of his danger.

It had all happened so fast. Lee had been at the back
of her mind for five of the most formative years of her
life. He had been the perfect man, a hero, and when
they had met again in Switzerland, his persuasive
charm, and his magnetic attraction had knocked her
sideways.

In the carefree mood of a well-needed holiday, she
had thrown off her hurt bitter skin and opened herself
up to love and romance, so sure that she could live the
careless, soulless life she saw all around her. The
trouble was that she couldn't. It hadn't been a brief,
no-strings-attached affair—she had fallen deeply in
love, sure when Lee asked her to marry him that he
must feel the same.

That stupid naïvety would be the death of her. Why
hadn't she known that cool hard experienced men like
Lee didn't marry for love? He was no romantic fool,
imagining the world well lost for love. He was a tough,
cynical, self-sufficient man who took what he wanted

from the world and was willing to pay the price. He would never fail or falter. He would always get what he wanted. He had needed a wife. He had desired her and had no doubt realised that she and Laurie would come together like long-lost friends.

He hadn't trapped her, she had walked into it of her own free will, blinded only by her own foolish romantic illusions. She had trapped herself in a watchful waiting life, where she slept alone every night and where she and her husband were like polite strangers, walking a careful slender tightrope, either one likely to fall to their doom at any time.

This is getting you nowhere, she thought, standing up with sudden decision. She smoothed down the pale wool of her dress and stiffened her spine. The facts were simple and couldn't be changed. She could either stay or leave and her decision was already made, not only because of Laurie but because that tiny flower of hope inside her refused to die.

The telephone started to ring again as she carried her coffee cup out to the kitchen. It was a woman with a soft breathless voice, asking for Lee.

'He's not here,' Marie-Claire snapped, sick and tired of being polite to husky-voiced females who rang for him. 'I suggest you try his office in London.' She slammed down the receiver with a grim smile of satisfaction. If she had to fight, she would fight dirty! But it was certainly a day for telephone calls, she thought, as she reached again for the receiver late in the afternoon. This time it was Becky.

'How did you get on with Chris?' her friend asked without preamble. 'What did he want?'

'It was awful,' Marie-Claire replied with a shudder. 'I didn't know what to say to him.'

'But why did he come?' Becky persisted curiously.

'I don't know—he kept on saying that his marriage was

a mistake. I wasn't really listening, I just wanted him to go.' She thought of the furious way Lee had reacted when he arrived home, the terrifying row they had had when Chris had gone.

'Poor you,' Becky said sympathetically. 'I think Chris regrets losing you, you know.' Marie-Claire hoped not. She had no desire to hurt Chris, but she certainly didn't care for him.

'Too late, I'm a happily married woman now,' she said lightly, the lie sticking in her throat. She couldn't even tell Becky the truth. It was locked inside her, a terrible secret.

'What's it like being married? Is it everything you expected? I haven't met that gorgeous man of yours yet. When are you going to invite me to dinner?'

Marie-Claire laughed at the bombarding questions, Becky's cheerfulness making her feel happier than she had done for days.

'Married life is great—you ought to try it—you'd like it, I'm sure,' she was repeating parrot fashion what she had said to Ran. Everybody asked the same questions, as though she had all the answers now, and could reveal some magic formula that could miraculously change people's lives.

'Chance would be a fine thing!' Becky replied, laughing. 'How about coming up to town next week? We could have lunch.'

'Lovely.' It would be nice to get away from the house for an afternoon. She had been too involved with her own problems over the past week or so to think of seeing friends. 'And I'll ask you to dinner as soon as I know what nights Lee has free next week, okay?'

'Yes, okay, but don't forget. I saw a photograph of him in the paper last week. Is he as handsome in the flesh?' Becky asked enthusiastically.

'More so,' Marie-Claire replied brightly, her heart turning over as she thought of him.

'I can't wait!' said Becky, making her laugh.

The snow began falling heavily again as darkness fell and Marie-Claire suggested that Mrs Ingram went off early. 'I can manage dinner,' she assured the housekeeper. 'It will be nice to cook a meal for Lee.'

'Well, if you're sure——' Mrs Ingram was obviously torn between doubt and eager agreement.

'Of course I'm sure. Look, I have to pick Laurie up from school, so I'll give you a lift home at the same time—the weather is getting worse,' Marie-Claire said persuasively, as she peered out of the kitchen windows. 'You don't want to be walking in this snow.'

So it was finally agreed, and she dropped Mrs Ingram outside her little cottage and drove on to the village school.

Laurie had been painting, her thin arms full of brightly-splashed rolls of paper, as she climbed into the car. 'Look!' she said excitedly, unrolling one of the paintings. 'It's me and you and Daddy.'

And it was. Three wobbly figures, the smallest in the middle, with names written in a childish hand underneath; 'Daddy', 'Mari-Clare', spelt wrong, and 'Me'.

'That's lovely, darling,' Marie-Claire said, sudden tears aching in her throat. Laurie thought of them as a family now, and that hurt. She knew that Lee had talked to his daughter, gently and carefully explaining the situation, but Laurie was strong-willed, already independent. She wanted to believe that Marie-Claire would stay for ever, that they were a proper family, like all her friends' families.

'Do you like it? Really?' Laurie asked as they crawled slowly through the thickening snow back to the house.

'Yes, it's very good,' Marie-Claire said definitely, concentrating on the road ahead.

'I did it for you,' Laurie told her proudly. 'Naomi never wanted my pictures, sometimes she didn't look at them.'

Marie-Claire bit her lip, her heart aching. Laurie mentioned her mother so casually, yet unknowingly she always gave so much away.

'Shall we pin it up in the kitchen so that your daddy can see it when he gets in?' she suggested, fiercely anxious to make up for the incredible fact that Naomi had never cared for her daughter.

'Oh, yes! Can we?' It was as though Laurie could hardly believe her good luck.

'As soon as we get in,' Marie-Claire promised huskily.

Later, after Laurie had eaten her tea, been bathed and put to bed, Marie-Claire sat down at the kitchen table with a cup of coffee, and wondered what to cook for dinner.

After a lot of deliberation she decided to play safe and settle for steak with new potatoes and fresh vegetables, followed by cheese and dark, sweet plums. And with the preparation completed, she took a quick shower, carefully made up her face and dressed in a pale green silk suit, taking great care with her appearance. She didn't know why she was doing it, she was driven by some crazy inexplicable impulse. Perhaps she was beginning to believe her own lies to the world, perhaps she was beginning to believe Laurie's picture of Lee and herself as a family, the perfect couple.

She set the table with extra care, placing fresh flowers in the centre, before checking the food. Everything was ready and she expected Lee at any minute, as he usually arrived home around seven.

The meat was practically ruined by the time she heard the roar of the car engine, over an hour later, and sitting alone waiting for him had sapped her already shaky confidence, and made the whole crazy idea seem just that—crazy.

She stiffened defensively as she heard him enter the room, and she felt so foolish in her soft silk and perfect make-up.

'I'm sorry I'm late,' Lee apologised, walking over to her. 'The weather is bloody awful—some of the smaller roads are blocked.' His cool grey eyes skimmed over her, and she tensed like a frightened animal, waiting for his amused contempt.

It didn't come. Instead he said quietly, 'Would you like a drink?'

She looked up at him warily. 'Sherry, please.' She licked her lips nervously. He was as distant, as remote as ever, she thought, watching him covertly as he poured the drinks. She stared compulsively at the powerful magnificence of his body barely disguised beneath the expensive tailoring of his suit, and drew a long shaky breath.

He handed her the sherry and sat down opposite to her, his hard face unreadable as he looked at her.

'You look beautiful,' he said with a slight smile.

Flustered by the betraying colour that ran beneath her skin at his compliment, she said too abruptly, 'The steak is ruined.'

'You're cooking dinner tonight?' he asked smoothly.

'Yes, I thought Mrs Ingram should go home— because of the snow, you see, and I thought it would be——'

'You don't have to explain yourself, Marie-Claire,' he cut in softly, his eyes dark with teasing amusement. 'This is your house, you must run it as you wish.'

'It's not my house,' she said quickly, but he ignored her, swallowing back his drink and standing up.

'I'm willing to take a chance on that steak.'

His voice was still teasing, but she was too tense to smile back at him as they walked into the dining room.

His eyes flicked impassively over the carefully laid table, the flowers, the shining silver and crystal, then he looked at her, noting the strained tension in her face, the wide wary darkness of her eyes.

Slowly he bent his head and brushed her mouth with his, smiling slightly at her surprise. He wasn't going to laugh at her, she realised with a pang of relief, as she served the slightly overdone food. He understood. And because of that understanding, she found herself able to relax as they ate.

Lee made her laugh, deliberately charming her, making it easy for them both. Marie-Claire felt herself responding to the magnetic pull of his charm, falling under his spell, unaware of her own gentle warmth and dark beauty, unaware that she was bewitching him.

After dinner they sat in the lounge listening to music, and Lee talked while she listened with rapt attention.

He seemed anxious to open his life to her, to allow her to get to know him better, and by the time she ran upstairs to bed, alone as she had been every night, she was smiling drowsily, so happy, she felt her heart would burst with it.

Tonight had been wonderful. They had actually spent time together without ending up at each other's throats! She remembered his dark caressing eyes and her heart lurched violently. Oh, Lee, I love you, she thought as she tiredly pulled off her clothes and slid into bed. She was asleep before her head touched the pillow, the light still on.

Two hours later, Lee leaned over her to switch out the light, staring down at the pale fragile beauty of her face in sleep. His shadow disturbed her, and she half-woke, murmuring his name. 'Lee . . .?'

'It's all right, go back to sleep,' he said huskily.

Marie-Claire turned to him, her eyes blinded by the light. She pushed her tousled hair from her eyes, unaware that her innocently provocative action brought his smouldering gaze to rest on the soft swell of her breasts, barely concealed by the thin satin nightdress she wore.

'Go back to sleep,' he repeated, his voice harsh now, uneven.

'Hold me,' she begged, still half asleep, unaware of what she was saying.

Lee swore under his breath. 'Goddammit, Marie-Claire, you don't know what you're asking,' he muttered roughly, but she was already asleep again, and despite his misgivings, the need to hold her in his arms overcame every other thought as he moved beside her.

He reached for her, gently pulling her warm slender, satin-clad body into his arms, and she turned to him, muttering his name in her sleep, resting her face against his smooth tanned shoulder. He stroked back the hair from her face, watching her as she slept so peacefully in his arms.

It was a God-awful mess, he thought wearily, and he would have to resolve it soon, or it would drive him out of his mind. He couldn't tolerate the thought of her with another man, with that drooling fair-haired boy he'd found touching her the day he picked Laurie up.

His arms tightened involuntarily around her, and she shifted restlessly, clinging to him. How long could it go on, this waiting, this strange limbo that was destroying them both? He couldn't let her go—he had thought of it, knowing that it was unfair to keep her, if she really was in love with her ex-fiancé—but it was beyond his power; he had never thought it possible to want a woman so much.

It was torture enough to hold her like this, when his body was aching with desire, his muscles clenched with iron self-control. There was still an innocence in her. She was a woman, she was a child, and she could drive him to the brink of insanity, to the brink of desire, with one look, one smile, one touch.

Finally he slept, and during the night Marie-Claire half woke again, and somehow it seemed sweetly and perfectly natural that her body was curved against the hard warmth of Lee's. Drowsily, she slid her arm around his waist, her mouth lazy as she kissed the hair-roughened skin of his chest. She sighed with contentment. This was where she wanted to belong. She couldn't sleep alone in this vast soft bed, she couldn't. . . .

She closed her eyes again, and wrapped in each other's arms, they slept until dawn, when Lee woke, sighing as he found Marie-Claire lying against his body, her hands clinging to him. Without disturbing her, he got up and took a long, harshly cold shower before dressing, a grim self-deprecating smile touching his mouth as the icy water pelted his taut body. He could almost enjoy the cold water against his skin, it left him feeling sharp and alert and ready to face another day.

Marie-Claire slept late, the exhaustion of half-slept nights finally catching up on her, panicking when she opened her eyes and found that it was after eleven. She sat up immediately. Laurie—school—the thoughts formed chaotically in her mind, until she realised that it was Saturday. She relaxed. Lee would have everything under control. Then she remembered that she had spent the night in his arms, which probably accounted for the fact that she had slept so deeply and now felt so refreshed. Her relaxation fled.

She jumped out of bed and took a hot shower. Lee hadn't touched her, he hadn't attempted to make love to her. It was a humiliating realisation. Perhaps he didn't even desire her any more. 'Without love it doesn't mean a damn thing.' His words echoed round her brain and she closed her eyes, letting her salty tears mingle with the water from the shower.

Half an hour later she was coolly composed, and made her way downstairs dressed in loose pink jeans and a matching cashmere sweater. The house seemed empty, but she found Mrs Ingram in the kitchen, cutting up vegetables for the soup she was making.

Greeting her, Marie-Claire poured herself some coffee and wandered over to the windows. It wasn't snowing now, but the snow on the ground was inches thick, blinding in the watery sunlight.

Movement just at the edge of her vision drew her attention and she turned her head to see Lee playing with Laurie in the snow. She watched them for long moments, her heart aching. Lee wore tight jeans and a short black leather jacket. He was smiling, his hard face relaxed, devastatingly attractive. Laurie clung to his hand, a brightly-coloured woollen hat framing her pixie face. It was a touching scene, one that Marie-Claire was completely isolated from, as she watched from behind glass. They were so close, the bond of love between them so deep, so untouchable. Surely any judge would see that. Lee was a good father, firm and gentle, and Laurie's open adoration as she smiled up at him twisted Marie-Claire's heart.

She turned away, absently responding to Mrs Ingram's chatter, feeling that it was wrong to intrude

by watching, and strolled into the hall, where the
morning post lay on a tall polished table. She flicked
through it automatically, not expecting to find
anything addressed to her, and came across a stiff
expensive white envelope addressed to Mr and Mrs
Lee Harper. She stared at it curiously, turning it over
in her hand. She was thinking how incredible it was—
to the world she *was* Mrs Lee Harper.

There was no hint who it was from, and with
sudden bravado, she ripped it open, to find inside an
equally expensive but informal invitation to a party.

It was from Naomi, primarily for Lee; her own
name was an obvious afterthought. She stared at the
delicate handwriting, a jealous dislike of Lee's ex-wife
stirring in her veins.

It began 'Darling——' and included the phrase 'Cal
and I'. Who was Cal? Marie-Claire wondered,
frowning. She hated the other woman's careless
intimacy, her body and mind revolting at the thought
of going to such a party. She could imagine just what
it would be like.

She heard Lee's voice in the kitchen and walked
through, still with the invitation in her hand.

Laurie was seated at the table, drinking hot
chocolate, swinging her legs. She greeted Marie-Claire
brightly, her cheeks a healthy glowing red.

Lee was drinking coffee, his grey eyes unfathomable
as they met hers. She felt herself flushing as she
walked towards him, memories of his smooth hard
body against hers, the heavy possessive tightness of his
arms, holding her through the night, taunting her, as
she suddenly remembered that it was she who had
begged him to hold her. Was he remembering too? His
eyes gave nothing away, his face, a hard blank mask.

'This came in the morning post,' she said, keeping
her voice carefully light. 'It was addressed to both of

us, so I opened it.' Why on earth was she explaining herself?

Lee took the card, his eyes skimming over it. 'Damn,' he muttered under his breath, his face hardening.

Marie-Claire stared at him. 'Who's Cal?' she asked curiously.

A cynical smile touched Lee's mouth. 'Cal Vickers, the multi-millionaire art collector whom Naomi married two months ago,' he explained laconically.

'Oh——' Marie-Claire sat down abruptly, her face mirroring her surprise. She had had no idea that Naomi had remarried. It had never even crossed her mind.

'Is that why——'

'She's bringing the custody case?' Lee cut in flatly. 'Very clever, my child. Apparently Cal Vickers is a family man—he has three children from a previous marriage. If Naomi is playing the doting stepmother now, it won't look too good that she lost custody of her own child. That's why she insisted on having Laurie at Christmas.' He glanced over at the child, who was oblivious to the conversation of the two adults, her head buried in a picture book.

'I can't let her win.' His hard expressionless voice sent shivers down Marie-Claire's spine.

'What about the invitation?' she asked cautiously

Lee shrugged his powerful shoulders. 'I guess she's heard about our marriage. She certainly won't have invited us out of the goodness of her heart.' His brooding eyes met hers, consideringly. 'Do you want to go?'

She half-smiled, feeling nervous. 'I don't know. I suppose we ought to, it might look strange if we don't.' She could see that he was reluctant. Why? she wondered. Because he knew that she could never match up to Naomi's beauty and undoubted style? Because everyone there would be comparing her with Naomi, and because she would come off second best?

Lee frowned heavily. 'They may give you a hard time, and I've little doubt that the poisonous Melissa will be there.'

Marie-Claire trembled inwardly, but pride raised her dark head. 'They can try to give me a hard time,' she amended, her eyes flashing.

Lee smiled, gently running a long finger down her cheek, but his narrowed eyes were still sombre. 'Naomi is a cold hard woman—she eats innocent young girls like you for breakfast,' he teased, but the warning note was there, very clear.

He was trying to put her off, she thought, but ignored it, gripped by a deep curiosity about his ex-wife. She wanted to meet Naomi. And because of Lee's obvious reluctance, contrarily, she now wanted to go to this party.

'I still think we should go,' she told him steadily. 'Surely it will help your case if you seem happily married, and if it's clear that you're going to fight for Laurie?'

Lee stared at her. 'You're such a brave child,' he said softly.

'I'm not a child, Lee,' she replied seriously, a little hurt.

She would show him, she would show Naomi and the bitchy Melissa. At this party, she would show them all!

CHAPTER NINE

MARIE-CLAIRE needed something very special to wear for the party, so she spent an afternoon scouring the shops of London with Becky, after they had lunched together.

In the end, she found what she was looking for in a tiny shop off Bond Street. It was perfect, expensive and outrageously chic, a three-piece outfit in black chiffon, the perfect colour for her dark hair and pale skin. There was a sheer petticoat worn under a skirt and loose matching top, both striped with glittering silver beads.

She tried it on tentatively, wondering if she had the courage to wear it, gasping at the pure slinky sensuality it gave to her slim body. It lent a dark fire to her eyes, the look of a sultry yet innocent temptress.

It was Becky's exclaimed, 'Marie-Claire, it's perfect! You look so sexy! You'll knock them dead!' that finally decided her, and she bought a pair of high-heeled black satin shoes to wear with it.

As she made up her face on the night of the party though, she had misgivings. She hadn't shown the outfit to Lee, she had wanted to surprise him.

Too late now, she thought fatalistically, and finished her make-up, then dressed, the thin chiffon and heavy beads cool against her heated skin.

She was brushing her hair when Lee tapped on the bedroom door. She felt her nerves tightening as she called, 'Come in.'

He strolled into the room, tall and dark and virile, also dressed in black, a powerfully attractive man. His eyes slid over her in slow masculine appraisal, taking in the shining softness of her hair, the translucent paleness of her skin and the stunning dress that turned her into a dark, beautiful seductress, an explosive combination that no man could resist. By the time his smoky unsmiling eyes returned to her face, she was flushed, her eyes huge and unsure as she waited tensely for his verdict.

'Dear God,' he said at last, his voice soft, very low. 'You look incredibly lovely—there won't be a man in the room who'll be able to drag his eyes from you tonight!'

Marie-Claire couldn't tell whether or not that was a compliment, and she was about to ask when he handed her a long flat velvet-covered case in silence. She opened it to find a heavy diamond bracelet, lying on a bed of soft satin. She smiled at him, her breathless pleasure shining in her eyes. 'It's beautiful—thank you! I've never worn diamonds before.'

'It will complement your dress,' he said, watching her with brooding intensity as she slipped it around her wrist.

Her fingers were shaking and she couldn't fasten it. She held out her slim wrist to Lee. 'Will you help me?'

She watched him as he walked towards her so indolently, towering over her, his cool hard fingers brushing the soft skin of her wrist as he clipped together the diamond bracelet.

Their eyes met and held in a moment of tense awareness and Lee bent his dark head, brushing her mouth with his own, the kiss deepening at her responding passion. He pulled her into his arms, lifting her so that her feet barely touched the floor as he tasted the innocent softness of her mouth. Marie-Claire clung to him, fingers stroking through his thick vital hair, trembling against the tense nape of his neck.

He released her reluctantly, his smouldering gaze lingering on the bruised outline of her lips. She swayed, dazed by the hunger she had felt in his kiss, and he steadied her, his hands hard against her shoulders.

'Let's go,' he said unreadably, and took her hand as they left the bedroom.

The party was at a huge house near Sloane Square, and was already in full swing when they arrived.

As they walked in, a woman moved towards them, detaching herself from the people she had been talking to, a breathtakingly beautiful woman in ivory silk that tightly wrapped and barely concealed the seductive, tanned perfection of her body. She had rich red curls that cascaded to her slim bare shoulders and the perfect bone structure that Marie-Claire recognised in Laurie.

So this was Naomi—much more beautiful and mystifying than Marie-Claire could have imagined.

'Lee, my darling,'—she tilted up her perfectly made up face and touched his lips with her own, 'I'm so glad you've come!'

Lee smiled, his eyes charming, his beautifully-moulded mouth curved. 'You knew I would, Naomi,' he responded smoothly. 'Is Cal here?'

'Of course he is, my darling—he never lets me out of his sight for a second—a lesson I wish you'd learned,' she complained huskily. 'And this must be your sweet little wife, Marie-Claire. I've heard all about you from Melissa.' She smiled charmingly, but her eyes were blank as they swept dismissively over Marie-Claire, lingering on the heavy diamond bracelet.

'How do you do,' Marie-Claire murmured politely but just as blankly. She could imagine what Melissa had said about her, and she *hated* Naomi on sight, even though she was knocked breathless by the woman's beauty.

Naomi was still staring at Marie-Claire's wrist. 'Your little wife obviously comes expensive, darling,' she said so sweetly, curving her long pale fingers around Lee's arm. 'Are her charms so spectacular?'

Marie-Claire watched the tensing of Lee's jaw, too shocked to say a word, as Naomi added softly, 'You must dance with me. I want to talk to you.'

Lee's eyes met Marie-Claire's. His were as hard and as cold as ice. 'Forgive me,' he said, with a slight gentle smile. She nodded, feeling sick, and watched as Naomi led him into the crowd, while she stood alone, hovering unsurely near the door.

She didn't know anybody at all as she looked round, and as the minutes passed and Lee did not return she began to feel slightly foolish in her dark slinky chiffon, aware that many curious eyes were resting on her.

Her pride rescued her. She wouldn't allow Naomi to make a fool of her, so she took a deep breath and pinning a brilliant smile on her face, she plunged into the crowd in search of a drink and perhaps a friendly face. The room was high-ceilinged, beautifully decorated, hung with paintings, and the people were well dressed, sophisticated, and not particularly friendly.

Unfortunately, when she found her drink, she also found Melissa. The other woman eyed her narrowly. 'So you came here with Lee,' she commented, openly malicious. 'Top marks for staying power, darling, but don't you feel just the tiniest bit de trop?' She shifted her glance, and following it, Marie-Claire saw Lee and Naomi, wrapped in each other's arms on the dance floor. Naomi's head was gracefully tilted up, she was smiling enchantingly into Lee's eyes.

Marie-Claire swallowed on the blockage of pain in

her throat. 'Jealous, Melissa?' she queried with acid sweetness. 'Isn't Lee paying you enough attention either?'

Melissa's mouth hardened. 'Why, you——'

'Shut up, Melissa.' Harrison had appeared beside them unnoticed, his voice cool as he cut off his wife in mid-sentence. 'Would you like to dance, Marie-Claire?'

She smiled her relief at him and said, 'I'd love to.'

Melissa's anger followed them as they threaded their way through the crowd. 'Well done,' Harrison laughed as they began to dance.

'For what?'

'Giving Melissa a taste of her own medicine—she was obviously stunned,' he replied with calm amusement.

'I couldn't help it, I just lost my temper. And besides, I didn't do very well, you know, I never can when it comes to smart replies.'

'You always think of them too late?' he suggested, and she nodded, laughing.

'You too?'

'Probably everybody. I must say that dress is really something.'

'Thank you.' Marie-Claire accepted the compliment graciously. Without wanting to, she found Lee and Naomi in front of her. They were laughing, Naomi still clinging to Lee as though she was drowning. Marie-Claire turned away, hurt beyond endurance, her mouth shaking. They were dancing like lovers. Harrison, staring down into her face, frowned, his glance following hers.

'Ah,' he said knowingly. 'Naomi.'

'She's so beautiful,' Marie-Claire whispered painfully.

'So are you.'

She raised her bruised eyes to his. 'You know what I mean—she's really beautiful.'

Harrison shrugged. 'I guess so, on the outside, but she's got no heart. Naomi is a beautiful shell full of ice. You're warm, Marie-Claire, you're kind and gentle, and Lee is your husband, not Naomi's—remember that.'

'I only hope she remembers it,' Marie-Claire said bitterly.

'Lee is not interested in Naomi,' Harrison assured her calmly.

'Isn't he? Look for yourself!'

'No, you look again and see it for what it really is. Naomi is putting on a show—probably for your benefit, because she hates to lose. You're the winner here, my dear, don't let her delude you with her games.'

Marie-Claire listened to what he was saying, willing herself to believe it, and smiled at him. 'You're so clever, Harrison, and so kind. I really don't know what I've done to deserve a friend like you,' she said gratefully.

'You're a baby in these shark-infested waters, Marie-Claire, you need a friend. But don't go mad with the flattery,' he laughed. 'I might start believing it!'

Half an hour passed slowly and she danced again with Harrison and a charming young man called Bob, then she stayed close to Harrison and the small knot of people that surrounded them.

She listened to the chatter, the talk of politics and the theatre, throwing in her own comments from time to time, but try as she might, she couldn't fling herself into the party mood. Even the gin she held in her hand didn't help.

She was tense and utterly miserable, her eyes

constantly scanning the room for Lee's dark head. There was no sign of him now, and no sign of Naomi. Where was he? When she thought of Naomi's beauty, she couldn't believe that Lee didn't regret losing her. Perhaps tonight he had realised his mistake in letting her go. Perhaps he had loved her all along, and had only married Marie-Claire to try and punish her, to try and bring her to her senses.

She tried to stop her thoughts, but they wouldn't be halted, before her eyes was the picture of them dancing together so intimately, their bodies fitting together so perfectly.

Parted lovers coming together again? The thought destroyed her.

Excusing herself, she made her way towards the open windows and the enclosed conservatory beyond. It was a glasshouse, darker and slightly cooler than the main room. Desperately thankful to be alone and away from all the frantic brightness and chatter, Marie-Claire relaxed the aching muscles of her face that had frozen into a smile, and wandered among the plants and shrubs, trying to pull herself together.

She sat down on a small wrought iron bench and closed her eyes. It was she who had wanted to come to this party, Lee had warned her that it would be difficult. She supposed she only had herself to blame.

She heard voices, soft laughter, coming towards her and opened her eyes again, stiffening as she realised that it was Naomi and Lee. She shrank back into the darkness, praying for invisibility as they passed—arm in arm, she noticed in sick dismay.

She couldn't drag her eyes away until she saw Naomi stop, a slender blur of pale silk swaying with deliberate and seductive provocation towards Lee. That was when Marie-Claire looked away. She gasped with pain, stuffing her hand in her mouth to keep silent, her imagination enthusiastically providing the pictures her eyes refused to look at.

The silence roared in her ears and she felt physically sick. Was he kissing her now? Was this a prelude to making love? All her worst fears seemed realised, everything she had hoped for falling around her ears in ruins. She had to get away.

In swift silence, she rushed stumbling from the glass conservatory and pushed her way through the crowded, unbearable party, stopping only to grab her coat and bag on the way to the front door. She saw Harrison briefly as she passed and knew he was watching her, wondering curiously. It didn't matter. It wasn't as though Lee was going to be worried. He wouldn't even notice that she'd gone; he was far too busy with Naomi.

A man who was obviously drunk tried to waylay her near the front door. She was rude, pushing his detaining hand from her arm and shooting past him. It felt like a nightmare until she reached the cold dark street outside.

It was raining, a thin bleak drizzle, and her breath clouded in pale gusts. She gazed up and down the empty car-lined street, looking for an empty taxi.

It Lee thought she was going to stay—if he thought she was going to allow herself to be humiliated by his blatant behaviour, he had another think coming!

A taxi shot past, and she raised her arm too late, missing it. Damn! she thought angrily, beginning to walk to the corner of the road, where the traffic was heavier.

Finally she managed to get a taxi, though the driver wasn't too pleased at having to go so far out of London.

Marie-Claire sat in the back, soaked to the skin as they sped towards the house, silent tears running down her face, a sick jealousy ripping her to shreds inside. And however hard she tried, the remembered picture of Lee and Naomi dancing together would not be banished.

Back at the house, she paid the taxi driver, adding a huge tip for which he actually smiled, and hurried inside. She walked through the silent high-ceilinged hall switching on all the lights, and knew that she had to leave. She couldn't stay now. If Lee wanted Naomi back he would ask her to leave anyway, and she couldn't bear the thought of facing that.

Without bothering to take off her coat, she ran upstairs and into the bedroom, her mind working overtime, running purely on instinct and impulse. She would leave now—before Lee had even noticed she was gone from the party. By the time he got home she would be miles away.

The house rang with silence and emptiness as she pulled her suitcase out of the wardrobe. Laurie was staying with her best friend Sandy for the night, and Mrs Ingram had gone home hours ago. Marie-Claire worked quickly and mechanically, throwing the bare essentials into the suitcase and wondering where to go. She finally decided on Becky, sure that her friend would put her up for the night, so that she could sort herself out.

The wet coat was very uncomfortable and hindered her speed, and in the end she shrugged out of it, realising as she caught sight of herself in the long mirror that she would have to change out of the black outfit. Strange that she could be so practical at a time like this, so damned practical!

She slid swiftly into serviceable jeans and a thick red jumper, flinging the black and silver finery over the back of a chair. And as she snapped shut the locks on the suitcase, she heard the ringing of the doorbell and froze in panic. Her heart was pounding; surely Lee wouldn't be back already?

The doorbell rang again, long and insistent, and she crept over to the window, trying to peer discreetly out of the curtains to see who was below. She couldn't see a thing. The night was pitch-black and there was no sign of a car.

It couldn't be Lee, she decided, trying to think logically. He would use his key, and besides, he always parked his car in front of the stone porch. She would have been able to see it from the window, she told herself anxiously.

The bell rang again and it was obvious that whoever it was outside had no intention of going away. She had to answer it, it might be something to do with Laurie. So, checking her face in the mirror—it looked pale and tear-stained, but not too bad—she ran downstairs to open the front door, only to find Chris on the doorstep—the very last person she had expected to see.

'Chris?' Her voice was high with astonishment. 'What on earth are you doing here?'

'Hi,' he said with a smile, as though there was nothing amiss in him turning up on the doorstep of Lee's house. 'How are you?'

Marie-Claire sighed impatiently. 'Look, Chris, I haven't got time for polite chit-chat. I'm on my way out.'

Chris looked at his watch. 'At this time of night?'

She frowned at him, thinking that she could ask him the same question. 'Yes, at this time of night. So if you don't mind——'

'I've got to talk to you,' he cut in, and his eyes were suddenly desperate. 'It's taken me all evening to screw up the courage to come here. Marie-Claire, for God's sake—surely you can spare me a few minutes, after all we shared together?'

She stared at him open-mouthed. 'Honestly, Chris, have you gone mad? It . . . It was all over long ago. Why do you keep coming here? If Lee finds you——'

'I know, I know,' Chris cut in irritably. 'Look, all I want to do is talk.'

Marie-Claire's mind was working fast. She had to get out of the house as soon as possible. Lee could be back at any time and she couldn't bear to face him. He had said that he would never let her go. After seeing Naomi tonight, he might well have changed his mind; either way, a confrontation would be unendurable for her.

Chris's unexpected appearance was a complication she had not bargained for, and although she felt utterly heartless, she really couldn't spare him any time right now.

She took a deep breath and looked at him, trying to form the words in her confused mind. He looked thinner, still as attractive, though now his attraction meant nothing to her, her heart filled with Lee's dark hard-boned face. Pain ran through her like fire as she thought of her husband and she had to force herself to concentrate on Chris.

'I'm not being awkward, Chris, or nasty, but I really have no time at all, not even a few minutes, to talk. I'm on my way to London and I'm leaving right away,' she said carefully, wishing that she hadn't had to tell him.

'London?' Chris looked at her, his eyes speculative. 'What's going on?'

'Chris——'

'Okay.' He held up his hands defeatedly, then smiled. 'Let me give you a lift.'

'No, I couldn't.' She had planned on getting the train. Her car was in the garage, but it belonged to Lee, bought with his money, and she couldn't take it.

'Why not?' he asked, an edge of belligerence in his voice. 'We're both going the same way. I won't pester you, I won't even say a word if you don't want me to. Come on, you've got nothing to lose—and I'd like to do something for you, to make up for—well, you know——'

He bombarded her with persuasion as she stood in the doorway, lost and alone and very hurt. She couldn't find the words to refuse and it was starting to snow again and she felt so tired and confused. She was wasting time. Lee could be back at any minute. The time was ticking by.

'Well, if you're sure it's no trouble . . . .' she began uncertainly.

'Believe me, it's no trouble. Are you ready now?' he asked eagerly, pleased because he had won, because she had given in.

'Yes, I'll get my case.' She turned away from the questions in his eyes. He was dying with curiosity and she knew what he was thinking. If she was leaving Lee, he could step in, turn the situation to his own advantage. He loved her, she realised numbly. And he had realised too late.

She felt sorry, because she had never wanted to hurt him, but she felt even sorrier for his new wife and their unborn child.

Chris was shallow and impulsive, his recklessness always landing him in sticky situations. His own pleasure was of paramount importance to him, he was used to drifting through life and taking what he wanted. Well, this time he had come unstuck! He was married, and Marie-Claire intended to remind him of that, insist that he take his responsibilities seriously. Even if she had still cared for him, she would have kept him at a strict arm's length, for his wife's sake. As it was, she couldn't even think of him as a friend.

She carried the suitcase downstairs. Chris was in the hall and he hurried forward, taking it from her eagerly. 'Chris——' she stopped him as he walked towards the door.

'Yes?' He turned, smiling.

'I appreciate you offering me a lift, but I don't want you to think——' She paused, not quite knowing how to get it across to him. 'What I mean is, you mustn't expect——'

'I know what you're trying to say,' he cut in quietly. 'And I don't expect a thing. You've made it pretty clear how you feel about me—about us——'

'Chris, there is no "us". You're married, I'm married. There's nothing else,' she exclaimed, almost irritated by him. 'I love Lee, I'll always love him—there will never be anybody else for me. Can you understand that?' She was close to tears, exhausted by the evening's events, by Chris's persistent hold on an idea that, in reality, did not exist.

But this time she seemed to have got through to him, for he stared at her, a certain defeat in his eyes.

'Yes, I can understand it. I suppose I thought——' He paused, shrugging. 'But you were never like that, were you Marie-Claire? You always believed in fidelity.'

'I still do,' she answered quietly.

'And that's my answer?' He had already given up, she realised with a sad relief. She had finally managed to convince him that she wasn't interested in anything he had to offer.

'I'm afraid so.' She softened the finality of it with a tired smile.

'Let's get going, then, shall we?' he suggested, almost cheerfully.

'I just have to collect my coat and my handbag—I won't be long.'

She left him in the hall with her case. She had to say goodbye to the house as well. Even though there had been little happiness for her here, it had become her home.

In the bedroom again she realised that she was still wearing Lee's diamond bracelet. She unclipped it, tears welling up in her eyes as she carefully placed it on the dressing table.

She looked around the room at the furniture, at the huge bed, where Lee had held her in his arms, and with a stifled sob, sank on to the quilted bedspread, suddenly crying her eyes out. She didn't want to leave the house. More than that, she didn't want to leave Laurie. And most of all the thought of leaving Lee tore her apart. But she had no choice. If she stayed, Lee would destroy her, her knowledge that he did not love her would destroy her. It had been the biggest mistake of her life and the future was bleak, filled with despair. But she knew for sure that given a second chance, she would make the same mistake again.

To have known Lee, to have been his lover, was the best thing in her life, despite the heartbreak and the misery. At least she would have some memories to keep her warm on the long lonely evenings of her future. She shivered, unable to face that empty future. She *had* to pull herself together. Chris was waiting downstairs. She had to stop crying and leave now, before it was too late.

She stood up, drying her eyes, washing her face with cold water in the bathroom before slipping on her fur coat and collecting her handbag. She looked a wreck, but she didn't care. Chris could interpret it any way he liked. All she wanted was to get to Becky's flat and go to bed.

She looked once more round the room before switching out the light and quietly closing the door.

She felt utterly wretched as she walked quickly along the landing to the stairs. She could never remember feeling more wretched or alone.

She heard the raised voices in the hall as though in a dream. She carried on walking, not understanding their significance until she reached the top of the stairs, where she froze in pure animal reflex at the scene downstairs.

Lee stood in the doorway, his dark overcoat emphasising the lean violent power of his body. Nearer the stairs, looking worried, flushed and disproportionately guilty, Chris clutched her suitcase.

To Marie-Claire's miserably detached mind it looked like a play being acted out below her. Her eyes were drawn to Lee, seeing only him, and the furious bitter anger that tensed his body. Why was he here? she wondered in confusion. Why was he so angry?

'Lee?' she whispered, forcing herself to move numbly down the stairs. The atmosphere was heavy with menace, with a waiting watchful violence.

Lee's grey eyes flicked coldly from the suitcase in Chris's hand to Marie-Claire huddled in her coat. She suddenly realised how it looked to him, how damning it seemed, how guilty they must look, caught in the act. He thought she was leaving with Chris. That was why he was so furious!

She laughed, for no reason at all, high hysterical laughter that echoed round the walls, cutting into the terrible silence.

Lee stared at her as she came towards him, and the expression in those narrowed eyes sent shivers of pure fear up and down her spine, raised the hair on the back of her neck. The high laughter froze in her throat.

He moved into the hall with furious cat-like grace. Chris backed away, dropping the suitcase, but Lee wasn't even looking at him. He was looking at Marie-Claire, his eyes merciless. 'Damn your cheating soul, Marie-Claire,' he bit out harshly, the cold words cutting into her like knives. 'Damn you to hell!'

She stopped, her feet faltering in panic. 'Lee——' Her mouth was dry, her throat aching with tension.

'Now look, Harper. . . .' Chris intervened weakly.

'Shut up and get out of here,' Lee said icily, not even turning to look at him.

Marie-Claire shuddered at his voice, staring at him in blind panic, so that suddenly, because of her fear, the mechanical actions of her body, her foot missed the stair and she felt herself falling.

She clutched wildly for the banister, but she was clutching at thin air, already falling, tumbling like a rag doll down the stairs. She knew nothing but fear, she heard herself screaming as though from a great distance. She heard Lee urgently calling her name, and she knew he was moving towards her at speed. But no one could save her. She fell quickly, hitting the floor at the bottom with a sickening thud.

Agonising pain shot through her jarring body on impact, and she cried out again as blackness blotted everything out.

CHAPTER TEN

MARIE-CLAIRE opened her eyes very slowly, very carefully. She had been awake for quite a few minutes, but she had kept her eyes closed, listening. There was no noise except birdsong.

When she did open her eyes, she found herself in bed, the light dim, but not dim enough to stop the stabbing pain in her temples. She groaned and let her eyes close again. She felt as though she was in limbo, her head full of painful grey cotton wool.

A hand touched her shoulder. Inside, it made her jump, but outwardly she showed no sign of noticing it. She felt as though she had no control over her limbs, her body was numb, not attached to her. There was somebody touching her shoulder again, and she had to open her eyes.

'Marie-Claire?'

It was Lee's voice, low and husky and—what? Worried?

She forced open her heavy reluctant eyelids, and found him leaning over her, his grey watchful eyes scanning her face.

She licked dry lips, wanting to speak. 'What happened?'

Lee's eyes shadowed with a bleak pain. 'You fell down the stairs, don't you remember?'

As he said it, she did. It all came back with painful clarity. It hurt, and she wanted the memory to go away. 'Are you still angry?' She could barely whisper. Her mouth felt like sand.

'No——' His long fingers gently touched her cheek. 'No, I'm not angry.'

'Can I have some water?' She stared into his dark eyes, then heard him moving. He lifted her head, aware that the movement made her wince with pain, and gently placed a glass to her lips.

She drank thirstily, feeling the coolness of the water flowing down through her body. Lee's touch was so incredibly gentle, she thought hazily, as he laid her back against the pillows, his fingers stroking soothingly across her aching forehead.

'How do you feel?' he asked quietly.

'I don't know. My head hurts,' she admitted weakly, giving in to the need to close her eyes again. 'I feel . . . tired.'

'Go to sleep.' His voice soothed her vague fretful thoughts.

'Stay with me——' She put out her hand, sighing when she felt his warm strong fingers closing around hers.

'I'll stay,' he promised, and his words had the power to let her fall asleep immediately.

When she awoke again, she felt much better. It was still dark, only a lamp illuminating the room with a soft dim glow. She stared up at the ceiling feeling strangely disorientated, but at least she felt human again and though her temples still ached, it was nothing to the throbbing pain of before.

She turned her head on the silken pillows and saw Lee. He was sitting at the bedside, idly smoking a cigarette.

Marie-Claire stared unnoticed at his hard shuttered profile, at the smoke curling from his lips, and emotion twisted deeply inside her.

'Lee. . . .'

He turned to look at her immediately. 'You're

awake!' He was on his feet in seconds, arching over her, his eyes holding hers, dark with concern. He hadn't shaved, she noticed inconsequentially; there was a tell-tale shadowing of stubble around his hard jaw.

'How do you feel now?' he demanded huskily.

She considered for a moment, then said, 'Not too bad. My body hurts—what happened to me?'

'Luckily you didn't break any bones. You're badly bruised and you hit your head. Alan checked you over and gave you a sedative.'

Alan Maynard was the local doctor, a firm friend of Lee's and a very good doctor.

'I don't remember,' she said, gently touching her head and finding a huge painful bump.

'It was a bloody miracle you didn't kill yourself,' Lee told her roughly.

'I'm sorry——' Marie-Claire shrank from his anger, weak enough to be intimidated by it.

Lee swore softly. 'Hell, no, *I'm* sorry. I shouldn't be shouting at you.' His wry gentleness turned her heart over.

'What time is it? she asked, peering at the closed curtains. 'Is it night-time? How long have I been in bed?'

'Twenty-four hours,' Lee replied with a tight smile. He looked at the gold watch on his wrist. 'It's ten-thirty.'

Marie-Claire looked at him, her mouth round with amazement. Twenty-four hours? She could hardly believe it!

'What about Laurie?' she asked anxiously, thinking that the child had to be picked up from Sandy's house.

'Laurie is in bed asleep,' Lee told her calmly. 'She's been hovering round the door all day, wanting to see you.'

Marie-Claire closed her eyes, feeling guilty. 'Could

I possibly have some tea?' she whispered, thirst still plaguing her.

'Of course. Are you hungry?'

His concern hurt her for some reason. 'A little,' she admitted cautiously, not wanting to cause him any more trouble than she had to.

When she heard the bedroom door closing and was sure he had gone, she opened her eyes again and examined herself with her hands. She felt stiff and she was badly bruised on her hip, her legs and her shoulders, but apart from that and the bump on her head, she felt all right, shuddering to think what might have happened. The long sleep must have cured her.

She pulled herself up against the high mound of pillows and smoothed back her tousled hair.

In the corner of the room, near one of the wardrobes, stood her suitcase, untouched, the suitcase Chris has been holding. . . . Her black and silver dress, rescued from the back of the chair, was on a hanger, hooked over the wardrobe door, and the diamond bracelet still lay on the dressing table, the glittering stones accusing her. What had happened to Chris? she wondered vaguely.

She felt confused, trapped as though time had stood still yet subtly changed, so that she was left in an unknown limbo. Lee was concerned, she could see that in his eyes, but she could also tell by his remoteness that he was angry—a terrible anger that he was deliberately reining in, probably because she was hurt.

She twisted restlessly into a more comfortable position, her eyes bright with unshed tears. She had no idea what she would do. The accident had changed all her plans.

Lee returned five minutes later with a tray in his hands. It held a pot of fresh tea, two boiled eggs and some thin, buttered toast.

'Eat it all if you can,' he said with a hard smile, placing it on her lap. 'Mrs Ingram's orders.'

'Thank you. Isn't Mrs Ingram——?'

'She's staying—she wants to help,' Lee told her expressionlessly.

She ate ravenously, finding her appetite, finishing everything on the tray and drinking two cups of tea before putting the tray aside and leaning back replete. She felt Lee's eyes on her, but ignored them, or tried to. When she glanced at him from beneath her lashes, she found his face hard, brooding, a muscle flicking in his jaw.

The silence suddenly became tense and rather frightening.

'What . . . what happened to . . .?' She realised it was the wrong thing to say, an incredibly stupid thing to say, before she uttered Chris's name.

Lee's eyes narrowed. 'Your ex-fiancé?' he queried coldly.

Marie-Claire was silent, lowering her head.

'I threw him out, and you'll be pleased to hear it was before I lost control of myself,' he told her grimly. 'I could have broken his bloody neck—I could have broken yours, if you hadn't been trying to accomplish that for yourself!'

Marie-Claire shivered, her hands nervously pleating the heavy bedspread. 'I'm tired,' she said in a small voice, cursing her own thoughtless stupidity.

Lee stood up immediately, his movements quick and angry, and strode from the room in silence.

She slept easily, partly because of her injuries and partly because the brief contact with Lee had exhausted her, and when she woke late the next morning she felt much better, almost back to normal physically. Mentally, she felt miserable and defeated. Last night Lee had looked at her as though he hated her, and that hurt like hell, lingering on in her memory like a dark cloud.

She lay staring up at the ceiling, reluctant to get up and face the day. It was the uncertainty that defeated her. Would he let her go today? She couldn't stay here, that must be clear to him.

A light tapping on her door broke into her reverie. She stiffened and called 'Come in,' sighing with relief when Laurie stuck her dark little head around the door.

'Are you awake yet?' the little girl demanded impatiently.

'Yes, I'm awake, come in and see me.' Marie-Claire couldn't help smiling at Laurie's impatience.

The little girl disappeared for a moment and when she returned she was carrying a breakfast tray. 'Mrs Ingram said I could bring it up,' she revealed proudly, 'She says we got to look after you. The flowers are from me—me and Daddy bought them in the village yesterday.'

They were a bunch of tiny early daffodils in a crystal vase with a crumpled blue ribbon tied around it. Marie-Claire thanked her with sudden tears in her eyes as she carefully placed the vase on the bedside table. The breakfast tray was meant to tempt her, holding hot croissants and poppy-seeded rolls, creamy butter, rich cherry conserve and a pot of fresh coffee.

'Are you better now?' Laurie asked worriedly, perching on the end of the bed, as Marie-Claire began to eat.

'I'm as good as new.'

'You were sick for a long time. Daddy wouldn't let me come and see you.'

'I was asleep, so I wouldn't have seen you, anyway,' Marie-Claire smiled.

'Are you going to get up? Can we go for a walk

together? The snow has gone, we could go to the river and——'

'Laurie, don't pester Marie-Claire.' Lee's deep amused voice made Marie-Claire jump.

She had not noticed him entering the bedroom. He was leaning indolently against the door jamb watching them both. Her pulses raced as she glanced at him, so lean and virile in denim jeans and an open-necked blue shirt.

'But, Daddy,' Laurie protested, her wide grey eyes innocent, 'I only wanted to know if Marie-Claire is getting up today. I miss her!'

Lee looked at Marie-Claire. 'I know, but you must let her eat her breakfast in peace,' he said gently.

Marie-Claire sipped her coffee. She had finished eating; Lee had taken away her appetite the moment he walked in.

'Okay.' Laurie obediently climbed off the bed. 'I'll go and help Mrs Ingram till Marie-Claire gets up.'

She smiled at them both and ran away, and in the silence that followed her departure, Marie-Claire could hear her singing as she ran downstairs.

'You look better,' Lee commented expressionlessly, walking into the room and coming to stand by the bed.

'Yes . . . yes, I'm fine . . . I think I will get up. . . .' she stammered, wishing that he would go away. He didn't move a muscle, merely watched her with a cool intensity that made her want to dive under the bedclothes for protection. Her nightdress was too revealing, thin green silk with slender bootlace shoulder straps, it barely concealed the soft thrust of her breasts, and left her smooth shoulders totally bare.

She felt naked under Lee's probing gaze, her hand moving to her throat in a gesture of unconscious modesty, her fingers resting against the pulse that beat so frantically there.

'Why the hell did you marry me?' he demanded suddenly in a taut voice.

Her head jerked up, her eyes meeting the furious depths of his for a second, before veering away again. What could she say? Because I love you, Lee, so deeply that I'm going to have to leave here before you destroy me? She could imagine his reaction to an admission like that. Would he laugh in her face, or would he perhaps treat her the same way he treated Laurie, gently but firmly? She almost laughed.

'I ... I....' Her mind was blank. She couldn't think of a suitable answer.

'Why, Marie-Claire?' he persisted coolly. 'For my money? Did you mean what you said to Raf Canovas? or did you marry me for revenge on your fiancé?'

'No!' she cried, unbearably hurt. 'How could you think that?'

He laughed, but there was no amusement in the eyes that remorselessly held hers. 'For God's sake, what else can I think?' he demanded grimly, moving nearer, his mouth cynical as he watched her flinch away from him. 'If I hadn't arrived back when I did, you would have left with him—without so much as a bloody word!'

'It wasn't like that....' she whispered, close to tears.

The dark brows rose. 'No?' he queried with bitter mockery. 'You weren't leaving with him?'

'No—yes—I——'

'Spare me the details,' he cut in harshly, his body tense.

'Why won't you let me explain?' Marie-Claire asked shakily.

'Because, dammit, I don't want to know about you and him. I can guess, all too well, what you're up to,' he replied implacably.

'Lee, please. . . .' She was begging for his under-standing, afraid of this tall angry man who was so cold, so immovable, so threatening. But he ignored her, coolly demanding, 'Where do you meet him, Marie-Claire? Here? Do you let him make love to you in my bed? What is it that you need—the excitement of an illicit affair?

'Stop it, *stop it*!' she cried, wincing with pain. 'It isn't like that, Chris——'

'Oh, I know all about Chris—I saw the way he was looking at you,' Lee grated tersely. 'He wants you, Marie-Claire.' His voice changed suddenly, becoming deep and silky. 'Almost as much as I want you. The only differnce is that I can take you, right here and now——'

Before she realised his intentions, he caught the bedcovers, flinging them back to reveal her silk-clad body.

'No——' she whispered hoarsely, her body beating with sudden unbidden heat as she saw the smoky desire in his eyes. 'Lee, no. . . .'

'Oh, yes, Marie-Claire,' he muttered softly. 'I've waited too long, night after night, while you were dreaming of him.'

'Lee, please. . . .' She was trembling. 'Don't make me hate you!'

His grey eyes held hers and he smiled. Her heart missed a beat. 'I don't give a damn if you hate me,' he responded quietly. 'You'll respond, Marie-Claire, you'll forget your hatred, you'll forget the man you love, you'll forget everything but me, and I'm willing to settle for that if it's all you have to give.'

He reached for her, his long fingers catching the neckline of her nightdress. And with one easy tug he ripped the silk from top to bottom, pushing it aside to expose her naked body to his glittering gaze.

Marie-Claire couldn't move a muscle. She lay hypnotised, her heart pounding, feeling the cool air against her skin, then the delicate erotic touch of Lee's hands as they swept possessively over her bare flesh.

He knelt beside her on the bed and she closed her eyes in defeat as his mouth hungrily parted hers, as he arched over her, his powerful body pressing her into the softness of the bed.

She tried not to respond, to lie passive, her heart breaking because it was desire that drove him, desire and anger, but not love. It was impossible. The fiercely possessive touch of his mouth awakened a deep answering need in her that matched and complemented the primeval electric driving force she felt in him.

She moaned softly in her throat, her mouth opening beneath his, her hands clenching against his shoulders.

She had ached with longing for him, she was starved of his touch, and her love was strong enough to block out his motives for making love to her, leaving them alone in the universe to express a passion that totally engulfed them both.

Lee's fingers were strong, hard-skinned, his touch erotically abrasive against her soft flesh. Marie-Claire gasped as he cupped her breasts, his thumbs brushing sensuously over her hardened nipples. His anger was gone, melting in the heat of desire as he held her, touched her, kissed her.

Somewhere deep in her mind, Marie-Claire knew that she should fight him, that she should resist the fierce power of his lovemaking, but as he kissed her, his mouth tracing fire over her skin, she realised that nothing mattered except this moment and the fact that she needed him just once more before she stepped out of his life for ever.

Lee's mouth was at her throat now, his tongue

erotically tracing a path to her soft shoulders, where his lips tenderly kissed her bruised skin. Fire roared in her veins, her blood quickening at his deliberately slow masculine dominance. She moaned in abandoned surrender as his lips moved lower to her aching breasts, his tongue flicking against her swollen nipples with delicate expertise. Her fingers tightened in the vital darkness of his hair to hold him closer, as she arched her responsive body to his mouth. She was already lost, aching with the tense spiralling heat of desire that he had aroused so easily. She clung to the hard unyielding strength of his body as his hands stroked over every inch of her, his hungry mouth following the path aroused by his fingers. And when his mouth finally touched hers again, capturing her lips with a burning heat, she opened her own mouth wide for a kiss that was endless.

'Touch me,' Lee murmured raggedly into her throat. 'Kiss me, Marie-Claire.'

She obeyed with a feverish enthusiasm, pulling open his thin shirt, pushing it from his wide smooth shoulders, her hands sliding exploringly over his powerful clenched muscles.

His skin was damp with sweat, the clean male scent of him, intoxicating her. She kissed his shoulders, delighting in her power over him, her hands flat against the rough hair on his body, then let her mouth drift tantalisingly down over his chest. His heart was racing heavily, beating up against her lips, and as convulsive shudders racked his body, she gave herself up to the deeply satisfying pleasure of touching him, of arousing him.

His body was hard and pure and magnificent. His skin tasted faintly salty, his stomach flat, the muscles unbearably tense as she flicked her tongue against the damp skin. Her trembling fingers fumbled with his clothes until he was naked beneath her hands, her gentle teasing lips. He groaned, shaking, tensing, as she made love to him, and her mouth moved urgently lower, using her sweet power to make him tremble, to make him groan with a need that made his breathing forced and heavy. His protest was hoarse when the pleasure became unbearable, and he pulled her up, lifting her yielding body against the burning heat of his arousal.

His hands stroked over her, gently moulding her flesh to his. His mouth touched hers and he moved lithely, so that she lay beneath him again, writhing, begging for his possession, as he pinned her to the bed.

Their bodies clung fiercely, damp with heat, and Marie-Claire's need for him was beyond anything she had ever imagined.

'Marie-Claire.' His voice was uneven, husky. 'Look at me.'

She opened her eyes reluctantly and stared up into his face. His bones were taut, his mouth compressed with desire, and his eyes were dark, almost black, probing into her very soul.

'Lee,' she groaned, not wanting to talk. She needed his love, his possession to ease the intolerable exquisite pain inside her. She looked at his naked shoulders above her, the smooth heavy muscles of his forearms as he arched over her, and shuddered.

'Do you love him?' he demanded. 'Do you, Marie-Claire?'

She stared at him, pained surprise stiffening her body, and icy coldness dousing the clawing heat of desire. She frowned. 'Lee, I——'

'Tell me, damn you, I want the truth,' Lee muttered remorselessly. 'Does he make you feel like this when you make love? Do you want him as you wanted me just now?'

Marie-Claire closed her eyes, terribly hurt and very vulnerable. She felt as though he had hit her.

'Let me go,' she whispered fearfully, shocked by his cruelty.

'Is that my answer?' Lee grated violently.

Her last defence against him was crumbling. Any minute she might humiliate herself by admitting her love for him, her desperate need.

'Yes,' she almost shouted, shrivelling with pain. '*Yes!*' She pushed futilely at his hard chest, his hair-roughened skin burning her palms. 'Leave me alone!' The tears were squeezing through her closed eyelids and she twisted restlessly beneath him.

Lee stared down at her with dark savage eyes, his breath coming sharply, heavily. Seconds ticked by too slowly. She couldn't bear to look at him. Then she felt him move off the bed, heard the faint rustling of his clothes as he shrgged into them.

She lay where he had left her, weak and stiff and hurting so much she wanted to die. She opened tear-filled eyes and stared at his chest, at his smooth graceful movements as he reached for his discarded shirt. Beneath his bronzed skin, the muscles rippled fluidly and despite all that had happened she could not drag her eyes away; she still wanted him.

He turned to look at her as he buttoned his shirt, his blank grey eyes sweeping coldly over her naked body. Hot colour ran beneath her waxen skin, but she couldn't move to cover herself.

There was a hard violence in his face. 'I thought I could take what I wanted from you, Marie-Claire,' he said grimly. 'But your cold duplicity defeats me. God, how can you respond to me like that when you freely admit you love another man?'

She didn't answer, turning away from him, pressing her face into the cool pillow, flinching with an agony that was unbearable. All the more unbearable because she had brought it all on herself. She had been so desperate not to expose her true feelings, terrified of rejection. But wasn't Lee rejecting her now, and wasn't this a million times worse?

As he turned away to leave the room, she stopped him, saying sharply, 'Well, while we're flinging accusations around, I might ask you the same question!'

'What?' He turned, his ominous blank gaze searing through her.

'I'm talking about your ex-wife!' Marie-Claire flung at him acidly.

His shoulders tensed. 'Let's leave Naomi out of this,' he replied dismissively, and walked from the bedroom without another word.

Rima came to see Marie-Claire two days later. She brought Ricky with her, and Laurie was immediately enchanted with the little boy, whisking him off to play in the kitchen.

'Thank goodness for Laurie!' Rima laughed as they drank coffee in front of the roaring fire in the lounge.

It was good to see Rima again, to hear her laughter, her carefree charm. By comparison, Marie-Claire felt dull and dingy. She hadn't seen Lee for two days. He had gone to Amsterdam on business, and although he was expected back that evening, for some crazy reason, she suspected that Naomi was with him.

Not that she had any evidence, but her thoughts ran riot and her imagination refused to be quelled. To her eternal shame, she had found herself on many occasions reaching for the telephone, caught between the dreadful urge to ring Naomi and see if she was in

London, and the even more desperate need to ring Lee's hotel in Amsterdam, just to hear his voice. She missed him dreadfully, with a hollow need she knew to be pointless. The house was empty without him, her life was empty, and she couldn't stop it from showing in her eyes. Even Laurie, with all her beauty and charm, couldn't cheer her up, although she would force herself to appear cheerful when they were together.

She and Rima chatted the afternoon away, talking about everything under the sun. Rima asked about Marie-Claire's fall, and revealed that she would be going with James to the Caribbean in a month's time. Her husband was needed on a big job and they would probably be away until early summer.

Rima's life was so full, so happy, Marie-Claire thought, unable to deny a little envy, and her marriage was so obviously perfect.

'When is Lee due back?' asked Rima, as Mrs Ingram appeared with a fresh pot of coffee and a plate of delicious-looking sandwiches.

'Tonight.' Marie-Claire tried to smile, but to her horror felt her face crumpling, the strain of pretending that everything was fine too much for her. And before she realised it, she was crying like a baby.

Rima watched in distress, handing her paper tissues and pouring fresh coffee, and when Marie-Claire had collected herself, she said quietly, 'Would you like to talk about it?'

The calm sympathy in her voice seemed to break Marie-Claire's barrier of solitude. She had to talk to someone, and she heard herself blurting out the whole story, from her arrival in Switzerland, after her break-up with Chris, to Lee's departure for Amsterdam.

Rima listened in silence, letting her get it all off her chest, then she said with certainty, 'Well, I can tell you for sure that Naomi's not with Lee in Amsterdam. I saw her myself yesterday in Oxford Street with the dreadful Melissa, and I'm sure you're wrong about her. Lee doesn't want her—not after what she did to him.'

'Tell me about her,' Marie-Claire begged. 'Lee never talks about her, and not knowing always makes me think the worst.'

'I don't know where to start—you know she was a dancer, a pretty famous one, actually, before she had Laurie.'

Marie-Claire nodded, her heart beating too fast, almost afraid of what Rima was going to tell her.

'I believe they met at a party, it was a whirlwind romance by all accounts, but it didn't last. There was talk that Naomi was pregnant when they married, that Lee was doing the decent thing. She's selfish and greedy—she wanted Lee's money, and as soon as she got her hands on it, she spent it like water. She wouldn't live anywhere except London, and by the time the baby started showing, the rot had well and truly set in. She blamed Lee for everything—the damage to her career, the pregnancy, the dullness of her life, as she called it. As soon as Laurie was born, she seemed to go wild. She was blatantly unfaithful to Lee. He would often come home and find the men actually in the house, and she neglected Laurie terribly, leaving her with the nanny Lee had employed, sometimes not seeing the baby for days at a time.' Rima paused, frowning, obviously disliking having to talk like this. 'Naomi is wild and very highly-strung with a violent temper. I think that Lee's apparently uncaring coldness goaded her into even more outrageous behaviour. Finally he divorced her, for Laurie's sake, I think—he was afraid that Naomi would damage the child permanently. He bought this

house and he and Laurie moved here. Naomi didn't
want the child—she made that very clear. She
disappeared abroad for a year and when the money ran
out, she began looking for another rich husband. Now
she's landed Cal Vickers, so she should be happy, but
this custody business over Laurie makes me think that
she still wants Lee. You see, I don't think she ever
really thought he would divorce her. She was relying
on her beauty, her charm, but Lee was obviously and
coldly immune. She hates to lose, and she's probably
furious that she's let a man like Lee slip through her
fingers.'

Marie-Claire listened in silence. Suddenly it all
became very clear—Lee's furious reaction to Chris on
the two occasions he had found him in the house.
Naomi must have hurt him badly, she thought, with
an aching heart. And then she remembered the party.

'He didn't seem at all immune to her at the party,'
she remembered sadly.

'You mean she got hold of him and whisked him
away?' Rima hazarded sceptically. 'Believe me, Marie-
Claire, I bet he did it for you. I've seen Naomi make
mincemeat of other women in public, and it's my
guess that you're not on her list of top ten people.
She's a bitch, and she doesn't care who she hurts as
long as she gets what she wants. I know that sounds
awful, but it's true.'

Marie-Claire sighed. 'It doesn't mean that he loves
me.'

'Do you love him?'

'Yes, I love him,' she admitted freely, her heart in
her eyes.

Rima smiled 'Then I'll tell you something—Lee
would probably kill me if he knew I was spilling the
beans! He told me in Switzerland that he'd met the
woman he wanted to marry. I could see it in his eyes,

and he was madly possessive of you. He was like a young man again, and we were so happy for you both. Perhaps this misunderstanding over Chris has made him draw back—could be that he's afraid to reach out for you. You're afraid of rejection and I think he is too. Naomi gave him a hard time, although he never showed it; she made his life hell until he divorced her. But he loves you, Marie-Claire, and I'm sure of that. So if you love him—well, you know what I'm saying, don't you?'

Long after Rima and Ricky had gone, Marie-Claire sat by the fire, mulling over what she had said.

If Lee did love her—and she didn't even dare to hope that he did—she had to tell him that she was in love with him before it was too late. She had to take the biggest chance of her life or she could lose everything. She had to find the courage, she had to tell him, even if Rima was totally wrong, and it wasn't going to be easy.

He arrived back before eight, strolling silently into the lounge where Marie-Claire sat alone, curled up in front of the fire, deep in thought.

He watched her through narrowed eyes, until, sensing his presence, she turned, her heart leaping into her throat as she saw him. She jumped to her feet, running a trembling hand through her silky hair.

'Can I get you a drink?' she asked nervously.

There were no greetings, no pleasantries between them, only silence and awareness and a dark electric emotion that filled the high room.

'Thanks.' Lee half smiled, watching her as she poured scotch for him and a small measure of vodka for herself.

'I want to talk to you,' he said unreadably as they both sat down.

Marie-Claire stared at him, unable to veil the

hunger in her eyes. His black hair gleamed in the overhead light, his tanned cheekbones held the sheen of polished teak. The expensive suit he wore emphasised his air of power and success, his self-assurance and magnetic virility. He looked cool and calm and very strong, while she was a mass of trembling nerves.

'I'm listening,' she said shakily, frightened of what he was about to say.

Lee's grey eyes held hers. 'I guess I've been avoiding this for too long and over the past few days I've been trying to work it out—there is no answer.' He paused, raking a hand through the darkness of his hair. 'What I'm saying, Marie-Claire, is that you're free to leave here whenever you want. I've been a bloody fool, I've been trying to hold you against your will—I guess I thought——' He broke off, shrugging. 'Oh, what the hell, you know what I'm saying.'

Marie-Claire kept her head down, her heart breaking. She knew exactly what he was saying, and Rima had been wrong. He didn't love her, he was trying to get rid of her. Naomi would probably be here five minutes after she had walked out of the front door, she thought bitterly.

In silence, she got to her feet. She didn't look at him, she didn't speak, but walked to the door in agony.

'Marie-Claire——' Lee moved swiftly, blocking her path.

The telephone began to ring, but both ignored it. Lee caught her chin, forcing her to meet his dark eyes. She looked up at him with painful defiance, trembling at his touch. 'Marie-Claire.' It was a soft groan. 'For God's sake——'

The door opened behind them. It was Mrs Ingram, flustered as she saw them so close, the atmosphere so overpowering. 'I'm sorry, Mr Harper. . . .' she began hesitantly. 'There's a telephone call for you——'

'Thank you, Mrs Ingram.' Lee's eyes held Marie-Claire's. 'I'll take it in here.'

He let her go reluctantly. She watched him move over to the telephone, dazed for a few seconds by his nearness. Then she came to her senses, and ran from the room, past the surprised housekeeper, and up the stairs to her bedroom, intending to pack and leave immediately. She tried to keep her mind blank because she knew that if she thought about it in any depth, the pain would be intolerable. As it was, she was hurting like hell. She had to get away before he destroyed her.

She was feverishly throwing things into a suitcase when the bedroom door opened. She knew it was Lee, but she didn't look up.

'You can't wait to get away, can you?' There was a hard edge to his voice, a deepness.

She was silent.

'That was Chris on the phone,' he revealed expressionlessly, watching the smooth grace of her body as she moved around the room.

Marie-Claire's head jerked up, flushing as she met his eyes.

'What did he want?' she asked as casually as she could. Lee's jacket and tie were gone, his waistcoat open.

'He told me that you don't give a damn about him. That he loves you, but that the feeling is definitely not reciprocated,' Lee said quietly.

Marie-Claire nervously licked her lips, feeling very vulnerable, as though all her skin had been ripped off, leaving her nerves raw and exposed.

'Why should he tell you that?' she mumbled, looking away.

Lee moved closer, and she backed away from him.

'Perhaps because he really does love you and he doesn't want to spoil your chances of happiness,' he suggested softly. 'He was anxious to explain everything.'

Marie-Claire frowned. So Chris had come to his senses at last. He was acting like the Chris she had once cared for, which didn't help her at all at that moment, because his explanation ripped away her last defence, her last barrier against Lee's indifference. Had Chris also revealed that she was in love with Lee? That would be the final humiliation, she wouldn't be able to bear it.

She searched Lee's face for some sign that he knew, but found none. 'Well, I'm leaving now, you'll be pleased to hear,' she said defiantly, as though he hadn't mentioned Chris.

'Is it the truth?' Lee asked deeply, ignoring her belligerent remark. She wanted to hurt him, she wanted to deny it, but tiredness and misery defeated her.

'Yes, it's the truth. I don't care for Chris, it was over between us before I went to Switzerland.'

'Then why did you lie to me?' His voice was low, carefully controlled.

'It was what you wanted to hear,' she retorted in pain.

'No!' He caught her arm, pulling her round to face him when she would have turned away. His fingers were strong, they burned her, branding her his possession for ever. 'I wanted to hear that you loved me—I wanted to hear you say it,' he said unevenly, his eyes darkening as he stared down into her fragile, suddenly pale face. His fingers tightened. 'It's no good, Marie-Claire, I can't let you go—not while there's the smallest chance——' He paused, shaking his head.

'I don't understand. . . .' she whispered, her throat aching with tension.

Lee smiled. 'No, my love, you don't.' He bent his dark head, his mouth touching the corner of hers. 'I love you,' he murmured the powerful words against her skin. 'I've loved you for five years—since that very first moment I saw you.'

'You . . . you love me . . .?' Marie-Claire echoed inanely, hardly daring to hope, hardly daring to believe.

'Yes, Marie-Claire, I love you so much it's tearing me apart,' he admitted huskily.

She felt as though she was about to faint; his husky admission melted her heart with joy, with a happiness that hurt almost as much as the pain she had been feeling before.

'But what about Naomi?' she asked, staring up at him.

'What about her?' Lee's mouth was impatient, his dark brows drawn together in a frown.

'After the party, I thought . . . I thought you wanted her back. . . .' Marie-Claire stammered, feeling foolish.

Lee swore under his breath. 'Dear God, I can't stand the sight of her,' he said, with a wry, half-angry smile. 'I was trying to protect you, that's all. I could see she was trying to get her claws into you—I was out of my mind when I found you'd gone!'

'I saw you in the conservatory,' Marie-Claire admitted, flushing.

'She told me she wanted to talk about the custody case. She suggested her bedroom, I suggested the conservatory,' Lee explained wryly.

'You must have loved her once.' She was defenceless, but she needed to know.

Lee shook his head. 'I wanted her,' he corrected slowly. 'And that soon passed. I know now that we would never have married, if Naomi hadn't been pregnant. I'd given up any crazy romantic notion that I'd ever find a woman I wanted to spend the rest of my life with—that is, until I nearly killed you that afternoon.'

Marie-Claire smiled tenderly. 'You were my hero,' she admitted guilelessly. 'I fantasised about you for ages——'

Lee kissed her, stopping her words, his mouth hungry, urgent, showing her the desire, the need he had been controlling so fiercely. Marie-Claire clung to his wide shoulders, matching his passion, her lips offering everything beneath the warm pressure of his, and when he finally raised his head, it was with extreme reluctance, his glittering eyes and taut body revealing his deep arousal.

'I know all about fantasy,' he said teasingly. 'You'd been on my mind for five years—I'd find myself unconsciously looking for you wherever I went, cursing myself for being all kinds of a fool for falling in love with a child. God knows, I couldn't believe it when you walked into the hotel, when I found out that you were Ran's cousin.'

'Fate,' Marie-Claire pronounced drowsily, moving closer against his hard body, revelling in his instant response.

'Fate? You wouldn't have anything to do with me,' Lee reminded her with a smile.

'I was frightened,' she admitted with shy honesty. 'I'd been so sure of people, then Chris had shown me that I couldn't trust myself, or anybody else, particularly men. I vowed from then on not to get involved, unless I was in control. I thought I'd be cool and sophisticated and have affairs. But when I was with you, I lost myself, I couldn't be cool or sophisticated, and I suppose I already knew that I was falling in love with you,' she smiled tremulously, 'again.' Lee drew her even closer, his mouth gentle against her forehead, and she sighed. 'I thought you didn't care, and I half believed Melissa because I was still so unsure of myself, and it had all happened so fast.'

'Dear God—fast?' Lee groaned. 'I seemed to have been waiting for you all my life, I grabbed the first chance I could to make you mine.'

Marie-Claire laughed, pure happiness running through her veins like champagne. 'You were angry,' she reminded him, sliding her arms around his waist, her hands caressing the muscled strength of his back. 'You rejected me.'

'No, my love.' He framed her beautiful face with his hands. 'I wanted you so badly it was like a nagging pain. I was crazily possessive, and I had to force myself to keep my hands off you. I thought you still cared for Chris, and that was driving me mad,' he said huskily, his eyes dark and serious. 'I was trying to face the fact that I might have to let you go.'

'Oh, Lee,' Marie-Claire whispered in sudden regret, 'I've wasted so much time——'

She was stopped by his mouth, warm, sensual and demanding.

'Tell me,' he muttered into her throat, his hands urgent.

'I love you,' she whispered against his mouth. 'I love you, I'll always love you.'

She felt him shaking as she spoke those words that meant everything. He lifted her into his powerful arms and carried her to the bed. He leaned over her, deftly removing her clothes before covering her pale slender body with the hard urgent strength of his own.

They made love with a white-hot molten need, a desperate hunger that drowned them both. When the

electrically shattering climax came Marie-Claire clung
desperately to the sweat-dampened hardness of Lee's
body, her nails raking his smooth skin. And in the
pleasure-washed aftermath, he held her possessively,
stroking back her tousled hair from her flushed face.

'God, how I love you.' His voice was drained, his
breathing still ragged. Marie-Claire stared into the
glazed darkness of his eyes and saw that love burning
there, a fierce all-consuming love that would keep her
in his arms for the rest of her life.

She sighed with contentment and laid her face
against his chest. She couldn't even remember being
so happy, it was almost too much to bear.

'We haven't had our honeymoon yet,' Lee
murmured, kissing her mouth. 'How do you feel about
the South Pacific?'

'Mm, sounds lovely.' She flicked her tongue against
the salty skin of his shoulder.

'Next week?' he groaned in response to her teasing
caresses.

'Yes, next week,' she agreed supremely happy.
'Dinner!' she suddenly remembered, in horror. 'Mrs
Ingram——'

Lee's smile was gentle. 'Forget Mrs Ingram,' he
commanded softly, then his voice changed, becoming
liquid, husky. 'I want you—slowly, this time.'

He reached for her, lingeringly kissing her mouth,
and she revelled in the abrupt tautening of his body
against hers. She responded hungrily, holding nothing
back, and in seconds, as his kiss deepened, she forgot
Mrs Ingram, she forgot everything but her love, her
need for the man who was holding her in his arms,
making love to her.

It was a need that would never be satisfied, a love
that would last for ever. She couldn't have asked for
anything more.